ON THIN ICE

Chesterford Coyotes 2

RJ SCOTT
V.L. LOCEY

Love Lane Books

Copyright

All Rights Reserved

On Thin Ice

A young adult hockey romance filled with making amends, family, friends, and discovering the real person inside while juggling the crazy, upside-down world of high school.

Jonah Robinson has really messed up. He's spent the last year hanging out with someone who wasn't leading him in a good direction. Now that Felix has seen the light, perhaps it's time for Jonah to do the same. Making amends is not going to be easy when he's not exactly been the nicest guy at Chesterford. With the help of his family and a special friend at the school, Jonah is ready to try to make things right with those he wronged. The first person on that long redemption list is Tyler, the brightest player on the Coyotes, at least in Jonah's eyes. He's taken a thousand pictures of Tyler for the school paper, but he's going to have to learn how to develop more than just negatives if he wants to grow close to Tyler.

Tyler Corrigan's dad has left, his mom is terrified he'll come back, and it's Tyler who's left to keep his little family in one piece. The only respite from real life is playing hockey, and he's an important part of the Chesterford Coyotes. Despite not being the biggest person on the ice, speed is his superpower, and the team has his back during the worst of the bullying he's had to endure. His friends make him feel safe when his real world is full of fear, but no one can protect his heart when an awkward and messed up Jonah—one of the worst of his bullies—is suddenly around every corner, wanting to make things right.

Sorry can be a difficult word to believe, but trusting your heart is everything.

Dedication

To my family who accepts me and all my foibles and quirks. Even the plastic banana in my holster.
VL Locey

Always for my family.
RJ Scott

ON THIN ICE

CHESTERFORD COYOTES 2

RJ SCOTT
V.L. LOCEY

Chapter One

Jonah

I WAS KIND OF DOOMED.

Actually, I was totally doomed. Like Dr. Doom was dropping all the doom he possessed—which was a lot—onto my head, and while it sucked, it was kind of expected. Still, I hated sitting at the kitchen table being chewed out by my folks as my siblings snickered in the living room.

"… cannot believe that you've been bullying people, Jonah. I know your mother and I raised you better. Look at me, Jonah. I want to make sure you're soaking in what I'm saying to you."

I raised my eyes from the bracelets on my wrist. My father's gaze met mine across the kitchen table, and what I saw in those dark brown eyes made me feel even shittier. He was not proud of me at all, neither was Mom, who was chewing on her lower lip, her light blue eyes worried and damp. I'd made her cry. Talk about feeling like something scraped out of my baby sister's diaper.

"I know it was wrong," I mumbled as I fingered the slim rubber bracelet with the bi colors on it. I'd slid it on just this afternoon, after seeing Tyler and his friends from the Gay Student Alliance working on decorations for the Halloween dance. A dance I was supposed to cover for the *Chesterford Chronicle*, the student paper, but that I wasn't allowed to go to because the principal had called my parents in for a conference. Seemed *someone* had dropped an anonymous note into the suggestion box outside the administration office saying that Jonah Robinson and Miles Brooks were using racial and homophobic slurs against other students. That had been the start of a really, awful, super-sized, monstrously bad day. And by the looks on my parents' faces, this terrible day was going to stretch into a craptastic week or month. Hell, maybe a year. I'd probably not see the outside world apart from school until I was sixteen.

I deserved it all though.

"Jonah, if you knew it was wrong why did you do

it?" Mom asked, pushing a strand of strawberry blonde hair behind her ear.

I wanted to explain that I'd overheard Mom and Dad talking about her job with Felix's family's company, about how losing her job would be a major hit to the family budget, how it worried them, how they wished they had something real they could hold onto.

I wanted to tell them the horrors of being bullied at my old school—that it didn't matter what school I was at, I never fitted.

I wanted to explain that this was why I'd hung onto Felix, and by extension Miles, just to keep myself protected, to keep my mom's job safe. Felix would go to bat for my mother if he and I were friends.

To try to fix everything wrong in my head.

All I could do was hang my head in shame.

"Peer pressure," Dad snapped, pushing to his feet to get another cup of coffee. It was his third in the past hour. He'd given up smoking two years ago and had substituted coffee for the nicotine. Mom had been giving him decaf for the past six months, unbeknownst to him. "Why stay friends with Felix and Miles? You had to know that no good would come of it."

I winced because it *was* all on me. I'd chosen to hang around them; it was *me* who'd put myself in that position.

Dad continued, this time with way more anger. "That damn Brooks family is a seething den of bigots. Remember the first time we went to the Chesterford Spring Carnival?"

"I remember," Mom whispered, her jaw tightening.

"Greg Brooks walks up to me, big as you please, and asks me if I had permission to be on the school grounds." Dad thunked his Carlisle Parks & Recreation mug on the counter next to the Keurig. "Does that man think that only White people are allowed to be on the Chesterford campus?" he asked the coffeemaker as he pawed in the big plastic container for the right pod. They were all the same, all green covers, but he dug around anyway, muttering to himself until he found the one that he wanted. The lone, red-covered pod amongst all the green. "Ha! Found one. Don't think I don't know what you're doing with the coffee, Emma."

Mom gave me a wobbly smile as Dad went off about the Brooks clan. "I know that there aren't many people of color on that campus, but to come right up to me and ask… why is this damn pot not making coffee?"

"Something probably plugged the needles. Let me fix it, just sit down, and talk to Jonah." Mom gave my arm a pat, then rose to poke at the coffee pot needles with a paperclip. Dad sighed and flopped down across from me, then gave me one of those long, sad looks of his.

"I'm so disappointed in you, Jonah. I know it's been hard to adjust to the new school. And I know we don't have all the cash falling out of our—"

"Terrence, language," Mom chided Dad. My younger siblings—three girls ranging from ten down to two—giggled out in the living room.

"Out of our pockets," Dad hurried to amend while the opening strains of *The Princess and the Frog* flowed into the kitchen. "I know it's been tough; I truly do. But you earned that scholarship in fine arts. You're an amazing photographer. Someday, you'll be out there snapping pictures for *National Geographic* or the *New York Times*."

Yeah, that was the dream. If only I could fix the broken parts of me.

"I know it was wrong," I said, again, and shame choked my words.

"Then why the hell did you do it? Why would you

hang around people who are bigots? Make us understand, Jonah. Make me see why a biracial young man would pal around with two hateful people like Felix Sinclair and Miles Brooks."

He sat back, arms folded over his wrinkled dress shirt. His tie was probably being worn by one of his daughters as a headband. Dad and Mom had been called into the principal's office after lunch, pulling them away from his job as the director of Parks and Recreation for Carlisle Borough and her new job taking orders at the local fast food drive-thru window, which was what she has been doing since losing her job at Sinclair Industries' main office. Both had been furious during that meeting. Furious, shocked, and ashamed.

"Felix has changed," I blurted out. Dad rolled his eyes. Mom made a sound as she poked violently at some plastic bit from inside the coffeemaker. "He has, honestly."

"Actions speak louder than words, Jonah. It's easy to say you've changed," Mom said, her jabbing of the plastic bit getting violent. Better the coffee basket than me. Mom was generally pretty chill, but when her only son acted like an asshole and she lost half a day's pay, she got crabby.

"No, Felix really has changed. He's dating Soren

Rowe now, openly, and they seem really happy. Only, he kind of isn't really talking to me and Miles anymore." My sight went back to my wrist, the band of rubber in soft shades of pink, purple, and royal blue feeling right on my skin. I'd never actually thought of myself as bisexual, not really, until I started on the school paper at Chesterford and had an epiphany. As the lone photographer on the *Chronicle* staff, I covered… well, everything on campus, and lots of off-campus as well. Sports included. Which was cool because I liked sports a lot. I played tennis and basketball, not on a team, but with kids in the neighborhood or my dad. It wasn't until I got to watch the Chesterford ice hockey team that I'd gotten into the sport. And then had the big bi wake-up call.

"That's good to hear. Soren and his fathers are good people." Mom finally got the coffeemaker flowing, the gurgles and hisses making Dad unclench. Soon they both had mugs in hand and were staring at me once more, waiting for me to say something brilliant. "I don't think you should associate with Miles anymore," Mom added, then took a sip of her coffee.

"Shouldn't have been hanging around him to begin with," Dad grumbled into his cup, sipping tentatively as Mom's head bobbed. "We know you're close to sixteen and feel the need to have your friends as you see fit, but—"

"No, no, I don't want to hang out with Miles anymore. I was never friends with him, but after Felix went off with Soren, he expected me to... no... I won't do it. He's just wrong, and I won't..." I couldn't think of what else to say. There wasn't any good in Miles, he wouldn't have a redemption arc in my life story.

Mom glanced at Dad. "That's good to hear. It's easy to get sucked into toxic relationships when you're new to a social group. But it's been two years now, and you should be able to mix into a wide range of friendship groups. You're smart, handsome, artistic, athletic, and funny."

"Takes after his father," Dad chimed in, his anger seeming to slowly be leaching away.

"That he does," Mom said, leaning over to peck Dad on his neatly trimmed, bearded cheek. "I hope you can figure out where you fit in, honey."

"Yeah, me too," I murmured, plucking at the bracelet I'd thieved out of a box the GSA had stashed inside the front doors. They were planning on handing them out to students as they entered the dance. "So can I go to the dance on Friday?"

"You're grounded." Dad gave me a look over his coffee cup.

"But it's for school," I wheedled, then glanced at my mother, only she wasn't backing down.

"Sorry, Jonah, but Mr. Wheeler will have to take the pictures for the dance. Being called into the principal's office is not a minor offense, nor is bullying people. Now, go to your room and do your homework. Your father and I will decide on how long your punishment will be."

I wanted to argue, but deep down I knew whatever they gave me would be justified. I'd been a fuck toad to some people who honestly didn't deserve it. I got to my feet in silence and pushed in my chair, my eyes on the tips of my sneakers.

"And, son, we expect you to apologize to everyone you hurt," Dad said, his words pulling my sight from my Converse. "I don't care if Felix or Miles do it or not, your mother and I raised you to be kind to people, and if you hurt someone, you say you're sorry. Isn't that right, girls?"

"That's right, Daddy!" Lana, Gemma, and Polly all yelled back in unison. Mom beamed, then frowned when the sound of shouting was followed by crying, then a feeble "Sorry" from Gemma. Mom pushed to her feet and exited the kitchen.

Dad gave me a firm look. "I mean it, Jonah. You make amends to the kids you hurt."

"I will," I whispered, rubbing my new bracelet.

I rushed my father, hugged him hard, then bolted out of the kitchen, through the living room to the stairs. Those I climbed two at a time, my vision blurry from unshed tears I did not want anyone to see. I burst through the door to my room, closed it, locked it, and then, stood in the center of my space as the tears ran down my cheeks. I dashed them away, unsure why I was even crying. The past couple of years had been hard.

So hard.

Being pulled from public school and dropped into a private school in my freshman year had been exciting. For about two days. Then, the differences between my middle-class family and most of the other families of the students at Chesterford had really started to show.

I could count on two hands the number of students at Chesterford who were BIPOC. There was one other Black guy on campus, Reggie Dunleavy, who played football and was the son of two plastic surgeons. A couple of Asian kids attended, and one Latina girl who was graduating this year, the daughter of Hector Manuel Rivera, the assistant mayor of Harrisburg and his wife, Elena, a corporate lawyer. Then there was me. Jonah Robinson, son of hard-working people with more love than ready cash, admitted to a scholarship program that opened the doors of private schools to the less fortunate. Of course, the wording on the application had been different, but that was the gist.

I toed off my shoes, fell across my bed, rolled to my back to stare at the poster of Johny Pitts, one of my idols. Johny was a biracial photographer and had made a name for himself in the UK doing a photo journey with poet Roger Robinson. They'd driven across the country asking *What Is Black Britain?* and the images and words from that trip were stunning. Someday, I hoped to be able to do something as meaningful as that for the world. Mom assured me I would, but it seemed so far away right now. I'd gotten off light at school, pulling three days detention for an admitted verbal battle Miles had gotten into while I'd hung back like a coward. I should have stood up for the kid Miles was calling a weak little sissy before giving the freshman a shoulder slam as he strolled away. I said nothing to Miles, but I did apologize to the kid before heading the opposite direction from Miles. I'd heard Miles shouting my name, but I had kept walking, and I planned to keep walking away from that kind of shit. Whether I found my crew or not. I just hoped I did find them soon. It was lonely being different…

I stared up at Johny as the sounds of my sister's singing along to "Almost There" filtered up the stairs. When Dad's voice joined the singalong, I had to tune out. Dad could not sing, like at all, but he sure thought he was the next coming of Snoop. Which he was not.

I found a playlist that I liked, pulling up something from one of my fave hip-hop/punk bands. While the family was jamming to Disney, I was listening to a trio of POC musicians singing about burning down the system, wondering if being biracial and bisexual was one too many bis for one dude to tote around.

I'd been drifting off when a soft knocking at my door pulled me from the hazy ether of in-between wakefulness and sleep.

"Jo-bah," Polly whispered under the crack of my door. "Jo-bah, lemme in peas."

There was nothing I could do, but let her in. There were times when my baby sisters got on my nerves, but overall, I loved them more than mostly anything on the planet. Aside from my parents, and our cat Linus. Oh, and my Kodak digital camera, purchased outright by me after working all summer at Betty Lo's

Creamery selling ice cream cones and milkshakes. Mom and Dad had been so proud of me for earning that money. Now, they thought I was a slug.

I am a slug. I'm lower than that. I'm just the same as the kids who'd picked on me at my old school.

I'm worse because I should have known better.

"Jo-bah, peas," my baby sister called, and so, being a dopey, smitten big brother, I left my bed and unlocked the door for her.

She gazed up at me, a drawing in her chubby hand, big brown eyes set in her tan, round face, her hair a wild mass of light brown curls no comb or brush could ever tame. All the girls had tight curls, same as me, I just kept mine buzzed because who has the time? Besides, I got cool designs in the clipped sides like lightning bolts, half-moons, spiderwebs, and stars.

"Jo-bah sad?" she asked as she handed the drawing up to me. "You crying?"

"No, I'm not crying, but I am kind of sad," I replied, examining the drawing. It was a brown circle with two black ovals that were maybe my eyes. Blue lines ran out of the black ovals, so possibly, those were tears? "Did you make this?"

"Uh-huh," she answered, skirting around me to dash into my room, then climb onto my bed. She flopped to her back—Little Mermaid nightgown twisted around her middle, her chunky thighs and calves exposed—and grabbed her toes. "I see Johny."

"Yeah, he's still there." I sat down beside her as she tried to stick her big toe into her nose. "Don't do that," I said, and she quit. For now. "Thanks for the drawing."

"You well-comb. Why you sad?"

I fell back on the bed to lie beside her. She giggled and cuddled in close to my side. The girl was a major cuddle-bug. I'd lost count how many times she'd left her toddler bed to come into my room to sleep with me—at least twice a week, if not more. I didn't mind. My bed was more than big enough for one teenager and one toddler.

"I did something bad," I told her, figuring that was enough for her.

"Oh, Jo-bah, why did you do bad things?" she asked as she rooted under my arm. I lifted it, and she snuggled into my side.

"I don't know. Why do you do bad things?" I asked, then glanced at her. She'd popped her thumb into her mouth, a sure sign she was tired. She shrugged. "Yeah, same here. But I won't do those bad things anymore."

Her tiny hand, the one with the free thumb, came

up to pat my face. "Jo-bah good boy forever now," she said—or I think that was what she said—around her thumb before her long lashes fell to rest on her pudgy cheeks. As she slept peacefully at my side, I pulled a notebook out of my backpack and opened it to a new page.

I had a list to make of the people I'd hurt.

And at the top of that list was Tyler Corrigan.

Yeah, I was doomed as doomed could be.

Chapter Two

Tyler

"… then apparently, so Maeve said, the parents were called in, and Miles got a five-day suspension."

"Not Jonah?"

"Yeah, but only three days for him…"

I tuned out the discussion of the latest gossip circling the halls of Chesterford. I had already dissected the whole suspension thing with Soren, who'd tracked me down as soon as he'd heard. He'd told me someone had anonymously turned in Miles and Jonah for bullying, and I didn't have the energy to summarize all the stuff in my head about any of them, nor about the complicated relationship I had with Felix, Jonah, and Miles.

Hell, I was barely handling the fact that Felix was talking to me instead of shouting at me. Him falling for my best friend was a kick in the teeth, or at least it had started out that way. What could Soren have possibly seen in someone like Felix, who enjoyed asserting his dominance by scaring people? Then, I began to see Felix through Soren's eyes, and suddenly, he was nothing more than a scared kid who didn't have a mom who cared for him, and slowly, the way Felix was with me had changed. We were kind of friends now.

"… heard that Jonah was all up in Miles' face telling him to leave a kid alone."

"Nah, but he apologized to the kid, told Miles they should leave."

The voices lowered then, but I could still hear. "Eva told Marc that it was the pink-haired kid who turned them in. Him. The one behind you. Don't look! Jeez, I said don't look."

"The one with lip-gloss and the rainbow pins?" the second voice asked.

"Yeah, the one who…"

I tried to tune them out, but it was as if I could feel the gazes of whoever was talking, and even though I wanted to turn around and say they were wrong, I didn't. It wasn't me who'd reported Miles and Jonah to the principal; it wasn't me who'd taken the video that had gone viral in the school and beyond. The one that had caught Miles shouting in some new kid's face, threatening him, calling him all kinds of shit things for his skin color, his size, accusing him of being queer like that was okay.

The video caught other things—like Jonah attempting to tug Miles away, Jonah apologizing to the kid after Miles eventually left him alone, and Jonah walking off in the opposite direction from Miles, his head down.

All of that spoke to the feelings I had for Jonah—that he was as stupid as Felix, and that maybe there was a good guy inside him, too.

"And you'll never guess what I heard about—"

I poked my earbuds in to drown out the talking, the cast of *Wicked* telling me that I needed to dance through life. Yeah, that would work well. Pink hair and lip gloss, plus a hint of eyeliner, was my go-to, but dancing in the hallways was so not happening. I'd save that for the bedroom or for when I was finally at college where I could be me all the time without being shamed for it.

A shadow fell across my books, and I sighed, hoping to hell it wasn't someone who wanted to talk to me because this essay on evolutionary principles wouldn't write itself. I waited for the shadow to leave, or move, or *something*, but it seemed like I was waiting in vain, and finally, when I couldn't ignore it any more, I glanced up.

Jonah.

My flight instinct kicked in, but eased almost immediately when I realized it was just Jonah and there was no sign of Miles. Talk about a Pavlov's dog-type reaction.

Jonah was mostly okay when it was just him, a bit of a dick for watching things go down, but okay when he was solo. Not that we talked, because if we were on our own, he would move away to avoid me, and then scurry off in any direction he could find. Only, here he was standing in the light and staring down at me, and I could see his mouth moving.

All I could hear was the chorus of "Defying Gravity", and I gestured to my ears to indicate the buds under my layered pink hair.

He nodded and indicated I take them out. Fuck. If I removed them, I'd have to talk to him, and I didn't have it in me to have a heated chat about whatever made Jonah look so determined.

He stared at me.

I stared back.

Then, with a sigh, I pulled out the buds and the song stopped.

"Hi," he said after a pause. I glanced past him, making sure Miles hadn't in fact made his way into the study room and was waiting to pounce on me. He'd already threatened me with payback for turning him in and said that in the less than thirty seconds he'd had before his father pushed him out of the main door.

I'll get you for doing this. That was what Miles had snarled at me. It didn't help that Miles' dad had sneered, snorted in disgust, and then, shoved his son in the back. The parting words from his dad were just as nasty as Miles were—the apple didn't fall far from the tree.

You couldn't take that kid out? Didn't raise you to be a freaking loser.

I knew all about shitty fathers, and for a moment, I recognized the hate in his father that meant maybe Miles never stood a chance. I knew how hard it was to fight out from under all the hate, but I'd had Mom, and she'd been my guiding light every single day of my life.

Maybe Miles' mom was as much of a loser as his dad?

He couldn't be more wrong about me making the

complaint—nothing good came from involving outside parties after threats of intimidation—just ask my mom. I had no idea who'd accused the two boys of bullying, given it was anonymous, but it definitely hadn't been me. If I thought it was worth bothering with, I would have reported things long ago, but I had knowledge of bigger bullies than Miles, and had terrifying firsthand experience of what happened when an aggressor was backed into a corner.

"And?" I prompted Jonah, who was bouncing on his toes a little, as if he couldn't stay still. I waited patiently, and when he opened his mouth a couple of times, just to shut it again, I was about done with waiting for him to talk and picked up the buds to continue my research.

"I'm sorry," he blurted, his dark eyes shining with emotion.

I could feel the gaze of all the students in the study room focused on whatever was going on here. I should have gone to the library—no one goes there to study except the kids who actually had to try really hard to do well in subjects. Now was the perfect time for me to make a big thing of him standing there; humiliate him, shout at him, rail at him for all the times he could have done more than just watch.

Instead, because I was so torn between

understanding and the hateful need for revenge, I deliberately replaced my earbuds and bent my head to the book open on the desk. He was still there. Still bouncing.

Then, he placed something on the corner of the desk and walked away. I refused to watch him leave.

He'd left me a candy bar, my favorite—Snickers —right there with a Post-it note stuck to the front. It held one word. *Sorry*.

Only then did I glance the way he'd gone, to find him watching me through the glass of the door, a hopeful expression demanding I acknowledge the weird-ass gift.

I nodded.

Then immediately pretended to go back to studying.

It was safer not to engage.

THE HALLOWEEN DANCE WAS ON SCHOOL GROUNDS, the large sports hall turned into a landscape of flashing lights and balloons. Even so, as soon as I saw that Miles was here, despite recently having finished his suspension, I probably shouldn't have gone to the bathroom on my own. I should have talked to a chaperone, or if I'd said where I was going, then Soren would have come with me, or Felix, given he'd appointed himself as the outspoken champion of all things protecting Tyler.

While Felix remained cautious around me, as if he were waiting for me to snap and demand he answer for all the shit he'd given me, he was also uber protective, and just a tiny bit annoying. Well, actually a lot annoying—I didn't need or want Felix watching my every move, getting between me and anyone who dared to look at me wrong. I knew he was trying to make up for the stuff he'd been part of, but his vocal and physical support was going so far the other way that it messed up everything.

It didn't help that my chest still tightened when Felix spoke to me, and I knew it was hard for him as he tried to make amends, but it was hard for me too.

My feelings are valid.

If someone hurts me, it's okay to freaking cry by myself, and to be scared, and to hide.

So yeah, I didn't ask either Soren or Felix to come with me because they were in the line for photos and were making this big statement about being together and *fuck everyone*. I came in on my own, and I was almost finished and back out, but as I headed to the sink to wash my hands, the door opened and shut, and the air inside the small space grew cramped with a prickling awareness. My chest tightened, and my shoulders hunched instinctively, and I hated that fear made me turn to check who it was.

I wish I hadn't faced the new arrival. It would have been better not to have known.

"The girls' bathroom is next door," Miles *asshole* Brooks sneered, his eyes glassy as the scent of beer hit my nose. Just him then—drunk, with his snarls and hatred of all things that weren't *his type*—and no sign of backup, which made the situation scarier. I wished that Jonah was with him, and I never thought I'd say that, but at least when Jonah was around, Miles stuck to words, and not actions.

And Jonah *had* given me the Snickers bar.

And he'd apologized.

I stared down at the sink, hiding my face behind the fall of my pale pink bangs—going turtle was my default position when faced with Miles, who was twice my size and a hundred times nastier than anyone else in this school. I'd learned that lesson early on—don't poke the bear.

"All alone?" he asked.

I refused to answer. Instead, I let icy cold water rush over my wrist, dampening the rainbow band telling anyone who didn't already realize that I was an ally, gay, or both, at any given time. When I'd gotten dressed for tonight, I'd felt beautiful when I added my armor—the pink hair, eyeliner, and the shiny lip gloss I wore, not to mention the flowing purple shirt and the ripped pants. I was a walking advertisement for the rainbow spectrum, always fighting to show the part of me that my father had demanded I hide.

I'd fought so hard it had nearly cost Mom everything.

My silence spoke volumes, and Miles probably thought it was fear, but he was only half right. The other half of my silence was self-preservation, and that was the part of this he hated. He wanted me to cry, or shout, or run—it was as if he needed me to do that. I refused.

"Hey, freak, I'm talking to you."

He hadn't moved closer, if anything he was keeping his distance, but I soon saw why when someone pushed at the door behind him, and he stopped it opening with a well-placed boot, becoming a barrier all by himself. He might not be near me, but it was just the two of us in here, and I was as trapped as if he'd gripped my arm and shoved me into the sink. I could almost taste the pain and the fear.

I won't panic.

"The door's jammed up!"

"Open the door!" someone yelled.

"Fuck off!" Miles shouted back with a snarl, and there was a clatter and muttering from outside.

"Someone get a chaperone!" whoever it was added, and then, there was no more banging or demands to be let in. Whoever it was had given up, left, not for one minute imagining I was in here with my nemesis, or at least one of them. At least they'd mentioned getting a chaperone to the door. Maybe I should have brought one of them with me to the bathroom. Maybe Soren's dads, big bad former hockey D-Man Jared, or maybe smooth-as-silk phenom Ten, both able to hip check men twice their size.

They'd be able to intimidate Miles into backing off, which would just delay the pain for later, but hell, I could deal with later over getting my head shoved into a toilet now.

"A chaperone will be here—"

"You're gonna pay for what you did!" Miles snarled and slammed a hand on the door.

I jumped, and he laughed, and the sound was that of evil spilling out of him, and I washed my hands, pretending I wasn't entirely aware of where Miles was standing.

I was over feeling as if something had been stolen

from me, and tears bubbled below the surface and made my throat tight. Why would anyone want to ruin the dance for me? What had I ever done to deserve any of this apart from being different?

"Leave me alone." I tipped my chin, going for confidence—and I was an expert in masking, but that didn't mean my emotions weren't knotted and tight.

"You scared, girly?"

"Is that the very best slur you can come up with?" I asked before I could stop myself, and I saw his muscles tense, the tic in his jaw, the way his eyes narrowed. Shit. I don't know what drove me to keep talking, but words spilled out of me in a rush, because words were a barrier that stopped people in their tracks. "It's kind of old now, right? I color my hair; therefore, I must be a girl."

"You *are* a girl," he said and laughed again.

I bristled. "You think calling me that is a slur? My mom is way harder and stronger than you, so it's not the insult you think it is."

"Yeah, right," he snarled, but then seemed confused.

I needed him to move away from the door, so maybe I could get around him. "About what I expected; you're not exactly a creative thinker."

His lips thinned and he took a step from the door,

his hands in fists, and I blindly reached to the left of me, looking for something to protect myself with. How much protection could I find while I waited for a chaperone to find me?

Keep talking, bamboozle him with nonsense.

"I mean, I admire your ability to simplify complex topics down to one word, and I'm sure that is a valuable skill that will serve you well in your future endeavors."

What am I even saying? Where is the chaperone?

"Whatever," Miles snapped—his standard reply for whenever I used words with over two syllables. I'm not saying that the only reason he passed exams was by cheating, or that his family bought their way into him having an education, but it was true.

I shook my wet hands and glanced at the drier, which I wouldn't use now, because if I did, I'd be in reach of Miles, who'd taken one more step closer. At least he was out of the path of the door, and if someone pushed it in, I could get out. He saw me checking out his position and smirked—rightly assessing I was planning to run, and I was probably scared.

Of course, I was freaking scared. I alternated between being brave and scared every damn day.

Someone banged the door, opening it enough to

knock Miles in the back, and he stumbled forward. I breathed a sigh of relief that it was one of Soren's dads, Jared, in the doorway, his grey eyes assessing the scene, taking in me, then Miles, and frowning.

"Boys?" he asked.

I didn't hang around, darting past Miles and evading Jared's outstretched hand, and headed out into the dance, right to the middle where no one could single me out. Soren was right there, Felix sashaying up close to him, and for a few moments, I reveled in having my friends near me.

Hell, Felix even smiled at me, and he was so high on life there wasn't a hint of his usual guilt. I liked when he smiled as if we were just normal friends. I needed that tonight. I ignored everything and gave myself time to think about all the good things, like Soren and Felix, and Jared hovering close enough to make me think nothing could hurt me.

Best thing to do was to forget Miles.

I WISHED I COULD FORGET MILES.

I'd tried so hard, but it had been a week since the dance, and every time I saw him I walked the other way. I'd already received three tardy slips, and detention was next because I was late to classes.

Teachers never noticed the repercussions of real life on students—or at least none of mine did. Not one teacher asked me why I'd dyed out the pink from my hair and gone back to my normal color, or why I was so quiet. Not even Soren had noticed that I was quiet this week, but then, he had Felix, didn't he?

Bitter, much?

What did I care? Since Miles had said he was going to make me pay, avoiding him was taking all my brain power. No one had come forward to own up to reporting him and Jonah, but the gossip had gone up a notch when a rumor started that it was Soren who'd turned them in. God knows who'd started the rumor, but Soren didn't take it well, and I sensed a storm brewing around my best friend. I was tense waiting for the explosion, and concerned about meeting Miles, and my head wasn't screwed on right at all. That was probably why I ended up in *entirely* the wrong corridor at *exactly* the wrong time, and walked straight into Jonah, who reached out to steady me, but wasn't quick enough to catch me.

My breath stopped—if Jonah was here, was Miles with him?

"Tyler," he blurted.

I retreated the way I had come, spotting Miles hanging around the art room and realizing my options were walking past him and his new group of cronies or dealing with Jonah. At least I had my hockey stuff to defend myself, and I knew exactly how to handle a stick, so Jonah had better leave me alone.

Chin up, shoulders back, I went with the lesser of two evils, turned smartly, and headed back past Jonah, calculating that if I cut across staff parking, I could make it to practice on time and not incur the wrath of Coach Sennett.

"You want to get coffee, or a hot chocolate, or something? With me I mean? So, we can talk?" Jonah said in a rush as he fell into step with me. What in hell?

I hurried my pace, but he was taller than me, and he kept level. "Go away." It was easy for me to say that to Jonah; I guess because without Miles—and before him, Felix—he was easy to ignore. Jonah had never threatened me verbally, or hurt me, he'd just been there backing the others up, staring at me with his soulful dark eyes and shutting down whenever I caught his gaze.

He was insistent on talking to me now, though. "Just five minutes to—"

"No." I upped my speed, deliberately letting my hockey stick tangle with his legs.

He stumbled as I got through a door and let it fall

back in his face. Then I sprinted across the parking lot and made it to the locker room with a few moments to spare.

"Cutting it close, Tyler," Shaun, our captain, commented.

"Sorry, got stuck with… stuff."

Shaun took the team seriously, but I did as well. Hockey was my safe place. No one on this team messed with me. No one said I wasn't good at my role on the wing alongside Soren. I wasn't big; I didn't hip check, I didn't fall on pucks, but you bet, if they needed a sprint-speed skater to sweep up the right, I was there, and I was fast.

I'd been a Coyote from day one, and thanks to the one thing I'd inherited from my deadbeat dad—my hockey skills—I was a valuable member of the team.

Felix caught my gaze, grinned at me just a little too hard, then winced when Soren elbowed him in the side. Even Soren was getting pissed on my behalf that Felix was still on edge with me, but it wasn't Soren's place to be concerned about Felix worrying about me. I wanted Felix's grin from the dance floor, the one that wasn't dripping with guilt, the one where I'd moved on, and Felix had moved on, and we could be friends. And I didn't want Soren trying to broker a new normal, because I already feared I was losing my best friend to his new boyfriend. We didn't hang out as much or talk as often.

Or was that me backing off because, subconsciously, I didn't want to be near Felix?

Probably.

Coach Sennett stepped into the locker room and all talking stopped as we waited for the usual practice instructions. Only he didn't immediately launch into what we'd be working on this session, someone else came in behind him.

Jonah was with him. Camera around his neck. Limping slightly. Hesitant, he scanned the room and didn't stop until his dark gaze settled on me. I thought I saw a change in his expression, not accusation over me tripping him, or anger that I wouldn't talk to him, but a thoughtful considering glance. He smiled then— a cautious, perhaps hopeful smile.

I mean, he was possibly smiling at all of us.

But he was staring at me.

What the hell?

Chapter Three

Jonah

JONAH, STOP STARING!

I pulled my sight from Tyler to find Felix scowling at me as if I were a cockroach that had darted out of the woodwork unexpectedly, which pissed me off because, before he'd found the light side of The Force, he and I had been friends. Of a sort. Not that I was evil still, nor ever had been. I'd just been... stupid.

"Okay, men, listen up. Jonah here is the staff photographer for the *Chronicle*. He's asked to spend time with the team to chronicle..." Here Coach Sennett waited for a chuckle, but got none, so he went on, "... a year on the ice for a display next spring for the Fine Arts Symposium that Chesterford co-hosts with the Greater Harrisburg Youth in Arts Project."

Everyone in skates looked totally unimpressed. Which I got. "Right," Coach sighed. "Well, he's gotten permission to be with the Coyotes from his student counselor and Mr. Wheeler from the paper, so here he is. Do what he asks. See you on the ice."

And off Coach went, his duty done. The team stared at me as if they were waiting for me to ask them to strike a pose. Tyler and Felix were incredibly tense.

"Okay, so." I ran my hand over my hair, my fingertips finding the stripes that Paul, my barber, had worked so skillfully into the sides of my hair. "What I'm looking for is nothing posed or set-up. I want to do a photo essay of high school hockey from the inside. What it's really like—the long practices, the crush of keeping up your GPA while being expected to practice and play at peak performance." The guys all muttered and gave me suspicious glances. Each of them was working their asses off to be noticed by scouts. Well, perhaps not all of them. Some were just here because they enjoyed the game, the camaraderie, and/or the way the hockey varsity letter looked on their jacket or college application. "I'll be dogging you guys for the season, snapping images of real life, nothing fake. I want to see the sweat, the blood, and the agony of defeat."

"Hey, no talking about losing in the locker room," Shaun quickly interjected as he stopped taping his stick. The others nodded. "Brings bad juju."

"Sorry, right, no talking about defeat," I hurried to correct myself, my guts knotting up tightly every time my sight fell on Tyler and Felix. "Just pretend I'm not here."

"That should be easy," I heard Felix mumble.

Soren gave him an elbow in the ribs. Then talk in the room shifted from me, thank God, to the upcoming practice. I removed my lens cap as I mulled over whether this idea was really as brilliant as I had originally thought it would be. A few days ago, after reading an online article about famous sports photographers, the idea had popped into my head. If I could get permission from the school and the parental units, I could be around the team. Being around the team meant being able to, hopefully, get close enough to apologize to Tyler. My first approach had been a spectacular fail, which I totally got. Of course, where the Coyotes were, Felix was too. He and I had fallen out of friendship, or whatever, which was fine, if that was how he wanted to play it, but at least have the balls to tell me to my face. Ghosting someone was lame.

"No taking pictures of my ass," Soren called out as he laced up his skates. The room broke into a round of chuckles, except for Tyler who was eyeballing me as if someone had dropped a rattlesnake into the smelly locker room. "Keep it PG-13 for my fans."

"I've seen your ass, Rowe. It ain't worth the film," someone from behind me shouted. Felix seemed tight, as if he wanted to say something snarky, but didn't quite dare. Which was how I felt most of the time now. Judged. Which I deserved.

"I'll have you know I have an ass that would stop a clock," Soren replied.

"What does that even mean?" Tyler asked, whipping his hair from his face only to have it swoop back down over his eye. It was a good look for him.

"I don't know. My grandfather says it to my grandmother all the time," Soren answered with a shrug.

I slid around the room quietly, taking pictures steadily, sometimes dropping to one knee or even to sit on the floor as the team readied itself for practice. As I lined up shots, checked for lighting, and crawled on all fours to get a killer picture of discarded skates resting on the rubber matting, I had a few minutes of pure artistic bliss. My mind was on nothing other than the images and the models. And that worked well until the guys hit the ice and my camera followed Tyler. Keeping the lens on him, I eased away from the high-speed skating drills to a corner of the rink, my camera locked onto Tyler. I wasn't wholly aware of being zeroed in on the boy with the wide smile and flicky hair. When he snaked around some cones on the ice like a speed demon, I lowered the camera and simply let his joy at being the fastest skater through the cones wash over me. His smile brought on one of my own.

Then Felix got into my face. I literally jerked back in surprise when my ex-friend skidded to a halt in front of me. Coach was telling a few guys to clear the ice of cones so they could practice shooting drills.

"If you're here to give Tyler shit, I won't let you do that," Felix snarled, his words low and menacing. Or would have been if I feared him, which I wasn't because I'd seen the new side of Felix, and he wasn't as bad a person as I'd thought.

"What, are you his personal protector now?" I asked, easing back until my ass met the boards. The sounds of young men goofing off filled the rink. Coach blew on his whistle a few times.

Felix glanced over his shoulder before leveling a look at me. "Just don't fuck with him," he warned as he tightened his grip on his stick.

"Hey, I'm not going to do anything as bad as punching him in the face. Which is what you did." Felix paled at the reminder. "Yeah, I remember that day. I remember all the times I watched you bully students who got in your way, so don't come at me with your new squeaky-clean holy-as–a-nun shit because I know just who you are."

"I'm not that guy anymore," he growled.

"I'm not either," I replied while standing my ground. "I'm trying to make amends." I glanced over at Tyler, and Felix frowned at me.

"With Tyler?"

"Yeah, with Tyler."

I thought he was going to say something else, but then we were cut off.

"Sinclair! You plan on joining the rest of the team at center ice, or are you too busy lining up your glamour shots?" Coach Sennett yelled at the top of his lungs.

Felix and I glared at each other. He skated off in a huff. My sight flew to the team kneeling at center ice around their coach. Tyler's bright green gaze was resting on me, his lips thin. Feeling like I'd been gut-punched, I shook it off. All of it. The shit with Felix, the wariness in Tyler's eyes, and the odd stares from the team.

"Glamour shot sign-ups are next week. Look for the form online," I called out, knowing a wisecrack would break the tension. It did. Some guys chuckled. Coach gave me a look that I took to mean stop being a putz, so I shut up, left the ice, and sat on the away bench by myself to sort through my shots. Most were pretty good, some were crap, but a few were amazing.

I studied one image of Tyler for a long time. I'd captured him after his goal, the tension he always seemed to carry on his face gone. His arms were up, his eyes shiny with joy. I wish he would even force a genuine smile at me but had no idea how to bring it out of him. Glancing up, I used my camera as a shield and took a few dozen more shots of the team interacting with Coach Sennett. My phone buzzed in my back pocket with an incoming text. My father was outside.

I stood, turned, gathered my bags from the locker room, and left the rink without saying goodbye. There was no one on the ice who cared if I was there or not. My pace picked up as I dashed over the frosty grounds to the waiting car. It was nearly dark now at five in the afternoon, the short fall days gripping the state tightly.

"You being chased or what?" Dad asked when I dove into the passenger seat, my backpack crushed between me and the seat. "I didn't know that ghosts of Chesterfield Academy roamed around the ice hockey rink."

Me either, but a few spirits of deeds past had run me out of the place with my tail tucked. Guess exorcising my past wouldn't be as easy as I had hoped.

OVER THE NEXT FEW DAYS, I PRETENDED TO BE THE spectral photographer to keep with the whole spooky spirit theme even though Halloween was over. Ghosting in and out of practices, being silent and unseen as much as possible to avoid any confrontations.

I was still grounded, but I did get a pardon for the school paper hockey project. Couldn't let my grades fall or my scholarship could be affected. So as long as I was trudging after the team taking snapshots, I was golden. The fact most of the Coyotes ignored me didn't bother me. Okay, yeah, it hurt badly, but I had no idea how to turn the page to my new story. Tyler kept his distance, while Felix hovered around him like some kind of freaky mother hen, feathers ruffled, barring me from trying to talk to the guy. The others did their best to play up and goof off for team morale, but even I could see that the guys were edgy. The issues with me, Felix, and Tyler had to be screwing things up in terms of morale.

On the Thursday before the first game of the season against Hershey, I was in the cafeteria eyeballing the mound of goulash on my plate as I moved through the line to pay. The place was packed with grades nine through twelve—as the lower grades had already eaten—but I faced eating a meal alone. Unless I wanted to sit with Miles, which was a big nope. I shuffled along, stopping to check out the desserts—fruit cup, brownie, pudding, or sugar cookie the size of a basketball—when someone slid into line behind me. The girl following me huffed, then giggled. I glanced to the left to see Soren Rowe at my side.

"Skip the pudding. It's got them little alien beads in it," he said to me as the blonde chick behind us batted her lashes. Which was a waste because Soren only had eyes for Felix. Period.

Why the hell was Soren Rowe talking to me outside the rink? As far as I knew, he disliked me.

Was this some sort of set-up? When nothing happened, I cleared my throat.

"You mean tapioca," I corrected while getting a sour look from the lunch lady in the hairnet who was in charge of desserts. Only one per student, please, unless you wished to pay extra was the rule. Since my lunch voucher covered the main meal, plus one dessert, extra anything was not happening.

"Right, that stuff. Nasty. Alien eggs. So, hey, if you're not already sitting with friends we have an empty seat at the Coyotes table." His smile was so big it nearly blinded me. It also rang my suspicion bell big time. I threw a glance at the table the hockey team was sitting at. They all looked back, ugly fake smiles on their faces. Tyler lifted his gaze from his dish of noodles and tiny meatballs, mistrust ripe on his face. "You're one of us now, right? Team photographer and all that." I nodded. "Then, I can say this without you coming unhinged. I'm not sure about you yet. I'm not sure about the way you treated other kids. No, I know, you're different now. I get it. Felix has made that same pledge and is working to right his wrongs. Totally cool with that. I just need you to tell me that you're serious about this change. I like Tyler, a lot, and I'm not really down with people hurting him. Not you, not my boyfriend, no one. So, this is just a little team chat from a concerned player to the team photographer. We cool about things?"

"Yeah, we're cool."

"Nice. You can move down the line now."

I scanned the table. No Felix. Huh. "Where's your boyfriend?"

"Oh, he had some oral surgery done today, so he's coming down from laughing gas as we speak. You should have seen his last text. He was telling me that he was some sort of cosmic paladin of love. Funny as hell."

I nodded, simply because I had no other response.

He stepped closer, his elbow now bumping mine, and I flung a look at him. His gaze met mine. "I'm sure he'll love you sharing that around," I commented, moved down the line, and handed over my lunch pass to be scanned. I was one of only a few on the school's dime. There was a younger kid, a Timmy something, who was in fifth grade, who was here through a different program for inner city kids because he had some sort of Sheldon Cooper brain when it came to math.

"Meh, he needs to loosen up a little," Soren said, giving the lunch lady a smile as he led me towards the Coyotes table with not-so-subtle nudges of his elbow to steer me from heading to a small table in the corner. "So yeah, totally digging the stuff that you're doing so far. Sit down next to me. Hey, guys, Jonah is here. Lucky I caught him before he went to sit with the art students."

Soren was really laying it on thick. The other players nodded and said hey or hi before returning to shoveling in their food.

"Hi, Tyler," I said as I unrolled my silverware.

"Hey," he replied softly, his green eyes flicking to me, then back to his food.

"So, tomorrow night, we'll be travelling to Hershey for a game in their barn," Soren opened with.

That, it seemed, broke the dam. The rest of the team started talking about how to beat one of the Coyotes' fiercest rivals, while I sat humped up eating some darn good goulash. This school had top-notch chefs. Nothing like the public school menus. Not that the food back at my old school was bad, but… well, it paled compared to the meals here. And that was all about the budgets, I totally got that, but my old school cafeteria made some killer pizza. So did Chesterford, but this place made pizza with spinach and olives and designer flatbread crusts, while my old school was straight up tons of cheese on thick doughy crust. I sure did miss that pizza.

"… of us when we get to Hershey?"

My attention flew from memories of old friends and chewy pizza crusts to the Coyotes. They were all staring at me. Crap. What had been said?

I swallowed my mouthful of noodle, then tried to say something smart. "Just be yourselves. This is a photo journal of the real world of scholastic ice hockey. Don't mug or anything, just do what you normally do, and I'll be right there to capture it."

Tyler got to his feet, his face pinched, and picked up his tray of half-eaten food. The others at the table stared at him in confusion.

"I have some work to do in the library," Tyler said, then left, dumping his food into the trash before hurrying through the cafeteria doors. I stared at him until he was gone from sight, the swinging doors making the social events posters pinned to a large corkboard on the wall flutter. My gaze went to the rest of the hockey players. They were all trying not to look upset, but the vibe at the table was decidedly shitty now.

"I should go, too," I said, rising to my sneakers.

"No, hey, man, sit," Soren said, appealing to the others at our table. "Tyler is just feeling off the past week or so. Sit, seriously, dude, it's all good."

The guys mumbled along, but I could feel the weirdness. Still, I sat back down, forcing the food into my mouth, as one by one, the group finished eating, then headed off to classes.

"Sorry, man, they're all wound up. This is a big game, and the locker room is cranky. But, in a way, I'm glad we have time to talk." Soren swung sideways in his seat as the cafeteria emptied slowly around us. The bell would ring in about five minutes to call us to our afternoon classes, mine being biology and my sole AP class, African American Studies. "So, part of the reason I wanted to have you here, other than you being part of the team now and trying to fix things with Tyler, was to talk to you about Felix."

That got my attention. "What about him?"

"Well, Felix is part of the issue with Tyler, and you…"

"And I'm the other." Not a question, just a statement of fact.

Soren shrugged. "Yeah, you are. And while I'm still pissed at how you acted; this BS needs to be resolved. It's affecting team morale, it's messing with Tyler's head, and it's making Felix act like some sort of moronic bodyguard. Tyler is a sensitive soul. He takes things to heart more than any other person that I've ever known. Which is cool and makes him unique, but the two of you circling around him like sharks has got to be freaking him out."

"You want me to drop my project?"

"No, totally not." He lifted both hands for emphasis. "I love your idea. What I'd like you to do, if you're willing, is to just talk to him like he's not breakable. I've already got it in my head to tell Felix to back the fuck off and let Tyler breathe."

"You want me to leave Tyler alone?" I was confused and felt like a turd. A bigger turd.

"No, I just wanted to float the idea of not looking at him like he brings you great sorrow every time you peep his way. Maybe try talking to him, instead of apologizing all the time."

"But I need to make him see that I'm sorry."

"He will. If you let him absorb the changes. I mean, you can tell someone that you've changed a thousand times, but that person has to *see* the changes. So just be you, give him space, treat him like the great guy he is, and he'll come around. And yes, Felix is going to get the same talk when he's not stoned."

The first bell rang. Chairs skidded across the tile floors as the lingerers stood.

"Okay, yeah, I can just be me. Give him space." I wasn't sure how not interacting with Tyler would show him I was sincere, but I was willing to give it a try. What I was doing now—long looks of great sorrow and regret—sure wasn't doing it. "If you talk to him, tell him that I really am sorry and I really am trying to be a good person."

"I think he knows that. You've said it often enough. Only good people care about the feelings of others. We all do stupid shit. Only the kind people try to make up for the stupid." He tapped my bicep with the side of his fist, then got to his feet. "Got to run. If I'm late for gym, Mr. Dalano will make me run extra laps around the gym, and I need to conserve that leg power for skating. See you at practice!"

I nodded at him. He gave me a stare, grabbed his tray, and took off for the side door that led to the gymnasium. I sat there for a long moment, staring at my alien eggs in a cup, unsure of what kind of cool, yet caring, tact I could try with Tyler

Maybe try dropping the tact and just be a nice guy. Let's try that.

Okay, yeah, we could go with that. Soon as I figured out how.

Chapter Four

Tyler

I HEADED STRAIGHT FOR THE LIBRARY—AWAY FROM Jonah and his hesitant smile, and the way he looked at me.

When he'd started at the school, I remembered thinking he was cute. A scholarship kid, he'd been a fish out of water, and he'd seemed shy. I had a feeling for him, just the one, a kind of protective wanna-be-friends kind of feeling, but nothing had come of it.

Maybe we could have been friends.

I loved the school library—huge oak shelving and a mess of nooks and crannies meant the library was my safe place, about the only spot where I could sit and study with no one to bother me. No one messed around in the library, mostly due to the beady gaze of Ms. Collymore, the resident librarian, who ruled the space with a rod of iron and saw everything. No one chatted loudly in the library, no one dared to mess about at all, no one took books and didn't return them, and she knew all of us by name. At least the kids who spent a lot of time in the stacks. I had a favorite table, right at the back in the corner, in the autobiography section—a desk big enough for one person to lay out their books and get ahead with homework in every available break, plus a leather chair so comfortable I'd often thought I might try to wheel it out under Ms. Collymore's nose.

"Mr. Corrigan," the voice was a whisper, and when I'd first heard it, way back, I'd imagined it was one of the infamous Chesterford ghosts, but soon came to learn it was only one snooping librarian who wanted to get up in my face about things.

At first, I'd hated her for all of the questions she threw at me. How are you? Do you need help? Is that a bruise on your face? Was that from hockey? Why was your mom crying when she dropped you off this morning… that kind of thing. It was as if she could see through the mask of pink hair and smiles to the hurt kid inside, and when the bullying had started, she'd been the one person I could rely on. One particularly bad day, she'd been the one to close the library door, barring anyone from coming in, so I had space to breathe.

"Hey, Ms. Collymore," I whispered back, and glanced up to see her with an arm full of books, smiling down at me.

"How did your geology project work out for you?"

"An A. Mr. Eghan said it was the best project on plate tectonics he'd seen." I'd been so stoked to get that plaudit, knowing how many hours I'd put into the work, and also, that it was a ton of research that had paid off.

"I'm so pleased."

"Thank you for your help in finding the resources."

"Always," she murmured, then juggled the books in her arms, sliding one onto my desk. "I think you might need this."

I tugged the book toward me, "environmental science and sustainability," I read out.

"That's the next component of earth sciences you'll be studying."

"Thank you." She inclined her head and took a

step away, but I called her name softly, and she turned back. "How do you know what's on every part of the curriculum?" It was a question I'd been meaning to ask for a while, but somehow this was the perfect opportunity.

"Who do you think they go to for resources themselves?"

"Google?" I teased, aware that the darkness from lunch was slipping away, one gentle encouraging smile at a time.

"Wash your mouth out, Mr. Corrigan," she teased, then vanished around the corner back to her desk at the front of the room.

My stomach grumbled; I wished I'd finished my food, but there'd been no Felix at the table, so I'd let my guard down, and when Soren invited Jonah to sit with us, I'd lost my appetite, which had now come back with a vengeance. What had Soren been thinking bringing Jonah over to us? It didn't make any sense at all. It was hard enough having Jonah at every practice, taking photos, chatting with some others on the team, and generally pretending to be all kinds of nice. I'd caught him smiling at me, and it made my chest tight.

Horribly tight.

I couldn't see good in him right now, and with

what I'd faced at home, I wasn't sure I ever would. It would take an incredible leap of faith for me to ever trust myself to talk to him, let alone smile back at him.

"Hey," someone approached me, and I stiffened and stopped reading. I knew that voice. I didn't want him here. I'd left the cafeteria to avoid him, and this was my safe space. I glanced up to see Jonah, his ever present camera around his neck, his dark eyes a hundred kinds of serious. He was holding out a banana to me. "You didn't eat much, and you left when I ... look... I didn't mean to... no... I just don't want you hungry... so I got you this."

I stared at the offering, then up at him, and back at the banana, waiting for what, I didn't know.

"Anyway," he whispered, as he glanced over his shoulder. "Don't let Colly see, okay?" I was completely aware that he was talking about Ms. Collymore. I knew that I was here at the desk and that there was a banana, but was this what an out-of-body experience felt like? He placed the yellow offering on top of the book that Ms. Collymore had given me. "Later."

I watched him leave. He didn't look back. If anything, he tripped over himself to get away from me, and disappeared down the side stack before I could even think to react.

What the hell was that all about?

Needless to say, I didn't eat the banana, got a warning from Ms. Collymore that there was no food allowed in the library, and headed off to my next class with an unsettled feeling of *what the fuck.*

I DIDN'T SEE ANYTHING OF JONAH BEFORE THE Hershey game. We didn't have classes together on a Friday, and then, there was a closed meeting before the game that the photographer extraordinaire wasn't allowed into. In fact, between the banana incident and the moment he caught my gaze from the seats by the Coyotes bench, there had been a Jonah-free zone—enough for me to get my head around the second offering of food. Or at least try.

I mean… what? I almost had affectionate thoughts about the gift… almost. After all, he'd given me a banana, and he tried smiling at me, and maybe that was something I needed to talk to a therapist about. I still saw someone every other week, a gentle man called Steven who'd attempted to unpick some of the things I'd seen and done. Secrets I would never tell anyone else.

"What's up?" Soren asked as we settled down next to each other. We were third line and wouldn't be out on the ice taking first shift. That was up to Shaun, our captain, with his wingmen and our first defense pairing, who were out there waiting for puck drop, which was less than two minutes away.

"Nothing," I said, focusing on trying to find my mom in the crowd of supporters, as opposed to worrying about Jonah and his freaking banana offering. I couldn't see her at first, but then, since Soren started at Chesterford and there was the slim chance his NHL-linked fathers would be here, it was difficult to find a seat, so much so that Coach had suggested ticketing, which seemed to amuse him. I finally found Mom, and I waited until she looked at me, and waved, something I always did, even when it caused Felix to sneer at me.

Not that he sneered at me now that he was good and shiny-in-love Felix, but still.

Then, I saw Felix's dad was right next to her, and when I glanced at Felix, he'd clearly noticed our parents together, too, because he caught my gaze and quirked a smile. I liked Felix's dad. James was a good guy, who took me and my mom in one night when Mom had gotten scared after a dropped phone call from my asshole dad. He'd probably been drinking and that was his go-to—freak out his ex-wife and son.

Sure, us being there had led to Felix losing his shit and hitting me, but Felix wasn't *that* person anymore. He'd said so. He'd said he was sorry, tried to explain about his mom, and all the vulnerable bits of him I kind of understood. Something of the uncertainty I was feeling must have shown in my expression because the cautious smile died in Felix's eyes. He broke the connection and focused on his stick tape.

Why did he get to look away from me as if *he* were hurt?

How did Jonah get to give me candy and bananas with that hangdog expression as if it was up to *me* to be nice back to him?

Wasn't it *me* who'd gotten punched? Wasn't it *me* who Jonah hadn't stood up for? Why couldn't Jonah have been a good guy from the start? Then, I would have been able to take the damn banana without feeling as if I was leaving myself open to hurt.

And fuck Felix with his self-pity and his rabid need to get between me and anything. Did he think *I* was broken? Did he think *I* cared about any of it?

By the time I hit the ice, I was mad at myself, at life, at a dad who'd fucked off, at Felix, at Jonah, at everything, and the white heat of temper gave extra fuel to my already fast skates. We didn't manage a goal this shift, but by the end of the first period, we were two goals up—one from me, one from Soren—and I was fully in the zone.

And it was easy to stay there as long as I didn't stare at Jonah.

Confusing, apologizing, staring-at-me, Jonah.

Chapter Five

Jonah

It was hard to not fill my camera with action shots of Tyler.

And not only because he was cute, which I'd finally admitted to myself about ten minutes ago when I'd snapped a shot of him on the bench talking with the guys on his line and smiling at something Soren had said. Sure, he was sweaty and grimy, and probably stank after a full period of skating full-bore, but there was something about the way his face was made. It was kind of perfect. And cute.

I'd lowered my camera when that realization hit home. Tyler was cute. And I was bi. Twice the bi. Funny how realizations kind of snuck up on you, then waffled you over the head like some cartoon rabbit with a huge rubber mallet. How had I not seen it before? I mean… okay, maybe I had noticed Tyler's eyes, lips, and smile, but I hadn't placed it all together in the CUTE file. Why had it taken so long for me to realize things other people knew from birth?

I shifted around behind the bench, my toes frozen, easing closer to the third line. Not to eavesdrop or anything, but to simply…. Okay, I was eavesdropping, but it was all for the project. I took a few shots of the coach, then angled a nice action photo of a crisp shot attempt, then a block by the Coyotes goalie, Rikki Peals. Rikki Roll as the team called him, then Coach would tell him not to lose that number. Which no one got other than Coach. Seemed it was some old song or something, who knows, people over forty are so weird.

Easing up behind Soren, I kept my camera to my eye and my ears open.

"… we can stop at the Salsa Palace on the way home," Soren was saying as the second period was winding down. "It's that place in Rutherford, but we have to win in order to get a taco stop."

"I love tacos," Tyler replied, his attention on the ice as he spoke. "Mom used to make them a lot. Really spicy ones with tons of sour cream."

Huh, my mom made tacos a lot, too. She and the girls spent all kinds of time in the kitchen on the weekends, making meals, then freezing them. I liked to help as well. Cooking made me feel good. Mom would smile at me over the heads of my sisters, then say something profound like: "*Cooking is love made visible*" or "*People who give you their food give you their hearts*," which was totally some Pinterest pins she had saved to one of her thousand boards, but it felt true. When you made food for someone, it showed you cared.

"*Yes!!*" the Coyotes shouted as they jumped to their feet. I jolted out of the food fantasy to see that the Hershey goalie had just let the puck soar past him into the net. The shot from Shaun a bullet no one in goal could have captured. Shaun had some real talent. Like collegiate or pro-level talent. And he was only a sophomore. Supposedly, NHL scouts were already sniffing around, comparing him to Tennant Madsen-Rowe, which was pretty massive praise.

The end of the second period sounded with a buzzer blast. The Coyotes were winning going into the third. We took a fifteen-minute break, the same length as each period of play, and during that break, I moved through the away locker room like the ghostly photographer once again. The idea of being unseen was that you got real life images. When people saw the camera, they tended to pose because who didn't want to look good in a picture? I slunk around the room silently, taking shots of Felix, who followed me with his gaze, Soren at his side as always, and then, I moved to the shadows to get a few shots of Coach pep-talking the guys. Then, as always, my attention strayed to Tyler, cute Tyler. I faded into the corner of the room even more when his bright green eyes found mine. The tips of his ears went red. My empty stomach flipped over on itself, making a knot in my gut that would make eating tacos tough. If we won. Which we did, with a goal from Tyler the Terror late in the third.

It had been such a pretty goal. A soft rolling pass from Soren that Tyler had picked up at center ice, then carried into the Hershey zone. Moving like the wind, he snuck a shot between the legs of a big Hershey defenseman, picked the puck back up, spun, and tucked it neatly between the pipe and the Hershey goalie's skate.

The bus ride back to Harrisburg was boisterous. When we pulled into the Salsa Palace in Rutherford Heights, everyone cheered. I lingered in the front seat as the team filed out, pretending to check my images. I'd not tried to move back. That was the team area, and despite the horseshit that Soren had shoveled at the lunch table, I was *not* the team anything. No one really liked me; they simply tolerated me. It hurt, sure, but it was to be expected. Making amends took time.

Once the bus was empty, I slipped out, bracing for the cold winds ripping through the parking lot. Hands in my coat pocket, shoulders around my ears, I jogged into the taco restaurant.

"You can sit with us," Coach said when I got in line. I smiled weakly at him and the volunteer coach, Shaun's dad, then added my order to the massive tab when I got to the register. If I needed proof that I was a troll among princes, I sure got it that night. Nothing says loser quite like having to sit with the adults while all the other teens were across the eatery joking and laughing and totally ignoring your existence. Guess that was what trolls who were trying to win over the villagers after eating a few kids had to go through, though. At least, I wasn't living under a bridge, so go Jonah's life.

THE FOLLOWING WEEK WAS LIGHT IN TERMS OF schoolwork, so I had lots of time to be grounded. Yay. Thankfully, there was a game against Ephrata on

Wednesday at Chesterford, so I was allowed to go to the campus, as long as I was outside the doors of the rink after the game ended. Which was fine with me. Not that anyone wanted to have me follow the team to Hot Pot Noodle Shop.

Dad dropped me off early because Dad was always early for everything. If a movie started at seven, Dad was in his seat at six-fifteen. And that seat had to be the last row on the left because, this way, no one was behind him kicking his seat.

So yeah, I was at the school an hour before I was needed. The campus was dark and cold, frost already settling on the grass as I hustled to the rink, my backpack bouncing off my back as my camera thudded against my chest. I'd brought my dinner, since Mom had been working a later shift at the burger joint and the game started at seven. I'd made a pot of Dad's famous chili, but since it was already late when he got home, it was barely done when we had to leave. I'd dished up a Rubbermaid container for myself, and one for Tyler because… food was love. Not that I loved him. That was absurd. I just thought he was cute, and I had to make amends to him. Maybe chili would do that.

The team began to file in about ten minutes after I arrived. I nodded at the guys. They nodded back, each carrying their own gear, their gazes not quite as dark as they had been a few weeks ago. Maybe I was making some progress with them. Of course, they weren't the ones who I'd stood by and let be bullied, so while it was nice to have less venomous looks, the one who mattered most still eyed me like I was a scorpion he'd found in his sneaker.

The door opened and blew in Tyler, as well as several dead leaves. He yanked it closed, spun, and saw me lingering next to the home locker room holding a container of food.

"Oh, hey," Tyler said warily as he hoisted the huge bag holding his equipment higher on his shoulder. He was windblown, his cheeks red, his hair all over the place. His cuteness rose one level. If only he would gaze at me with something other than distrust. Just once…

"Hey, so, I made dinner tonight and thought this might be tasty." I held out the container, then realized I had brought no silverware for him to use. "Crap, hold on." I shoved the chili into his chest, the container bumping the skates hanging over his shoulder, and dug into my backpack like a frantic mole. "I probs have some plastic cutlery in here. Mom always takes home a few handfuls from work." I realized what I had said and blanched, my sight flying to Tyler as I rummaged around in my backpack. "Not that she steals or anything. She brings home food for dinner sometimes and throws in lots of napkins and extra silverware because my sisters always drop theirs on the floor. The back seat of Mom's car looks like a silverware graveyard with Barbie shoe sprinkles."

Tyler smiled. A real smile that made his green eyes glow like hand-polished emeralds. My empty belly twisted tighter as my dick decided now was the time to wake up and stir around in my briefs. I wanted to fucking die. Thank God, my winter coat was long enough to hide my embarrassment.

"That's funny," he confessed, his smile fading as he must have noticed who he was smiling at. Then, the corners of his mouth straightened while his brow furrowed. "Why do you keep bringing me food?" he asked, and hey, it was a legit question.

Wished I had a good answer. One that wouldn't sound like a wooden plaque hanging on the kitchen wall. After twenty seconds passed and I said nothing, I blurted out the solo thing that was rolling around inside my head.

"Food is love," I answered. Tyler's eyes rounded. "Mom says," I tacked on as panic threatened to make me toss the baggie containing a spork and napkin at

Tyler, then race off into the night howling in embarrassment. "Mom says that food makes everything better. So yeah, chili that I made with beans. Don't eat the beans if you don't want. My little sister Gemma has a bean screen, Dad likes to tease. She picks out all the beans, then feeds them to my dad, which Mom asks her not to do because Mom has to sleep with Dad."

Tyler stood there, mouth slightly open and eyes wide, staring at me as I blathered on about my dad's bean farts. The earth could open up and swallow me right now, and I would be totally down with that. "Not saying that you fart or anything because, hey, maybe you don't. And if you eat that, and you do stink out the locker room, then that's… uhm… well, it's kind of funny right?" He blinked. "Cool, yeah, so I'm going to go and do…" I jerked the spork in the direction of the ice. "Take some ice pictures. Yeah, lots of ice pics. Totally makes the ice hockey connection even more… connected."

I placed the spork and napkin atop his container, backed up, and took a step towards the seats that I planned to crawl under and live forever like the troll that I was. Maybe I would charge people a toll of one candy bar to get to their seats.

"I like the beans," Tyler said, his expression

shifting from confusion to something softer... maybe? I was about to say something—it would have been stupid anyway—when Soren and Felix arrived with shouts and bitter winter winds. They hustled inside, laughing and holding hands, then froze when they saw the great chili charity event taking place in front of them.

"Oh, hey," Soren said cautiously.

Felix bristled.

I rolled my eyes and walked off, leaving them to be best buddies or whatever it was they were doing.

"Jonah?" Tyler called. I stopped, inhaled to steel myself against the dislike surely coming my way, and glanced back over my shoulder. "Thanks," Tyler said as a brief, shy smile tugged at the corners of his mouth.

I inclined my head in a super cool way, then walked to the ice feeling much lighter than I had in years. Maybe Mom was right, and food *was* love. Or like. Even trolls could like a cute guy, right?

Chapter Six

Tyler

IT WAS REALLY NICE CHILI, THE KIND THAT DIDN'T quite blow my head off, but was spicy enough to make my tongue burn. It might puzzle me as to why Jonah gave me chili, but that didn't mean I was confused about eating it—I was a growing boy and ate everything in sight, or so Mom said. Added to that, hockey was intense, and I used up a lot of energy, which was why on top of the chili, I was now eating a second dinner—my mom's chicken parm.

"… and then the trustees finally admitted it's airtight," she finished, and sat back in her chair, a cloud of relief around her. "And that's the last thing tying your father to us."

I nodded, much as I had been doing through this entire conversation. She'd lost me when she started explaining the legal side of the prenup my dad had been made to sign before becoming part of the Corrigan family. My grandparents hadn't thought much of Clive McAdams back then, hence the prenup, which saved the family fortune from falling into his hands, which sounded kind of dramatic, but was true. Not that I had any idea what my grandparents thought of things now, given my mom had cut all ties to them a while back.

They'd been proponents of letting Clive stay married to Mom, stay as my dad—they didn't seem to care he was abusive, or that he made our lives miserable. As far as they were concerned it was all about saving face.

We weren't super rich by any stretch of the imagination, but my grandmother considered herself as being blue blood and had enough invested in her social stock that, to her, appearances were everything. She didn't want anyone to see that the Boston Corrigans weren't anything but perfect, and that included closing my mom down when she threatened to go public with what my dad had done to her, and by extension, me. In a very rare moment of passion, my grandmother persuaded Mom that out of sight was out of mind, and promised she'd find a way to ensure he wouldn't worry us anymore.

I hated that he was still out there, not paying for what he'd done, and I hated that he still had the influence to make Mom blanch every time there was a dropped call, or that fear of him meant she barely left the house, apart from going to watch my hockey games.

"Aren't you hungry?" she asked, and I glanced at my plate where I'd been pushing chicken into a pile in the middle. Then, she pressed a hand to my head. "You're not hot."

I rolled my eyes at her with affection. "Jonah made me chili, and I ate it after hockey."

She frowned, then paled. "Jonah who… Felix's friend… the one who…"

She couldn't get the words out, knowing the weight of them.

"He was never the super bad one," I said in Jonah's defense. Why was I defending him?

"He still scared you."

To Mom, that was the framework of her life. She'd been scared so often that everything she did was imbued with tension. She jumped at the slightest noise; she worried about me all the time; and she hated herself for it. Only recently had she seemed to smile, and I put that down to Felix's dad, who'd shown her nothing but kindness. So much so that I wondered if maybe they might start dating, which would make me and Felix dating-in-laws, which I knew wasn't a thing, but still, it was a big switch around from him taking his frustrations at life out on me.

"I think he's trying to make amends, or friends, or I don't know."

But he keeps staring at me, and there's something of the boy I first met when he started at Chesterford. The shy, bright-eyed artist was back, with his hesitant smile. I'd liked *that* version of Jonah, had thought we might be friends, hell, for a few seconds, I felt the tug of attraction. Way back. Before Felix. I felt my mood drop instantly, and just like that, Mom could tell something was wrong.

Mom took the stool opposite—we always ate food at the counter in the kitchen and never in the formal dining room.

"Is he doing it the right way?" she asked after a pause.

"Is who doing what the right way?" I'd gone down a rabbit hole of thoughts and lost the thread of what we'd been talking about.

"Jonah. Is he making amends the right way, or is

he making you see things that aren't there? Is he being true?" She was asking the right questions—Dad had tried frequently to get back in our lives by saying he'd turned a new leaf. Was that what Jonah was doing? A sudden chill ran down my spine—was Jonah being truthful? I hadn't even thought about that, but was he going to do a dad on me and turn on a dime?

Not everyone is your father. My therapist's words filtered into my brain. The key messages he'd always wanted me to cling to were that my dad's shortcomings weren't my fault and not everyone out there has a nasty streak like he did.

I thought about the answer, then sighed. "Well, he seems to think the way to forgiveness is to feed me. So far, I've had a banana, candy, and a bowl of chili that he says is made of love or something." I hadn't followed everything he'd been saying, too busy staring at the scarlet that brightened his cheeks when embarrassment tripped him up and watching the emotion in his dark eyes.

Mom was quiet, meeting my gaze steadily, and I squirmed in my chair. She was using the mom look, and I wasn't sure why.

"You like him," she said.

I ignored that because I didn't know what I felt

about him. "Do you think, maybe, he's just confused about life? It can't be easy being the odd one out at school, y'know, the scholarship and everything?"

"Just promise me you won't do anything stupid like make excuses for someone who never stood up for you?" she said with a concerned expression and a smile that didn't reach her eyes.

Is that what I was doing? "I won't."

YESTERDAY'S FOOD GIFT FROM JONAH HAD BEEN three miniature bags of Haribo Starmix, with a Post-it note that said he'd chosen the ones that had the most fried egg-shaped candy for me.

How did he know they were my favorites? I loved nibbling at the yellow part, then finishing with the white, and I thought only Soren knew that. Unless Soren had told Felix who told Jonah, which was why I was now confronting Soren and trying to ignore the fact he wasn't taking this seriously.

"Just answer the question."

He pasted on a serious expression. "No, I didn't tell Felix that you like those freaky little Haribo eggs, and I'm sure, even if I did, that he wouldn't have shared this vital information with one of two people he goes out of his way to avoid."

"Well, somehow Jonah found out," I said.

Soren shrugged. "Lucky guess?"

Maybe the eggs *had* been nothing more than a lucky guess, but when Jonah dropped a red velvet cupcake decorated with vanilla icing and sprinkles on my desk in study period, I reached my limit.

"How do you know that this is my favorite cake?" I demanded loudly before he could back away to make his escape.

He blinked at me, and I was lost in his eyes again. Jeez. What was wrong with me?

His gaze raked me from head to toe, and he blushed. "Your pink is back." He pointed at my hair and ignored my question completely.

"And?" I snapped. "Am I too *gay* for you?" Wow, where had that come from?

"No! I like it, sorry, I uhm…" He turned and scurried off so fast I had no hope of catching him, given the entire contents of my backpack were spread out on the desk.

"What was that all about?" Courtney asked. We'd gotten about half way through study period, and I'd been so engrossed in what I was doing, I'd clearly forgotten she was there.

"Jonah keeps feeding me," I said as I pointed at the door he'd left through.

She rested her chin on her hands. "Tell me more."

I glanced at the people around me. It was only Courtney and a kid from my AP Math class who was seriously lost in working out whatever meant he had three calculators on his desk. I leaned in; she leaned in.

"He says he's sorry, and food is the way he's doing it. I mean, look at these!" I pulled out the three bags of candy.

She reached past me to snag one of the packs of Haribo, opening it and handing me the egg, which of course I took—I wasn't so confused that I'd turn down perfectly good candy.

"I guess it's better than interpretive dance." She snickered and reached for the cupcake, which I eased out of her reach. No one touched the yumminess that was a red velvet cake with vanilla icing.

That thought of Jonah dancing in front of me was horrifying. "I mean it. What does he want me to do? Because he's freaking me out."

"Meh," she began with a shrug. "He's not the same since Felix did his one-eighty and fell for Soren and became Mr. Nice Guy," Courtney observed, then bit the head off a tiny jelly baby, "and you're only freaked out because you used to like Jonah way back."

"I did not."

She fluttered her lashes, "Oh, Courtney, have you seen the new boy? He's so preeeeetyyyy." She did a very good approximation of exactly what I'd said to her when I first saw Jonah. Damn her and her freaky memory. "You were smitten," she added.

"I was not."

"Were too."

I threw a bag of Haribo at her, which she caught and pocketed with a wink. Great. *Now, I've lost two packets.* I pushed the third one into my backpack for safekeeping away from sneaky friends and edged the cupcake a few more inches out of her reach.

Just in case.

"YOU'RE GOING TO BE LATE."

I stiffened when Jonah said that from behind me, catching me unaware. I'd hovered by my locker for a while now, lost in thought, and mostly deciding whether to go the long way to hockey or chance the shortcut that might put me in the way of Miles. The same Miles who *still* refused to believe that it wasn't me who'd shared the damn video or turned him in to the principal.

"No, I won't be," I lied.

Jonah checked his watch. "You will. Coach Sennett is very firm on—"

"I'm the one on the freaking team; I know all about Coach Sennett." The implication being that Jonah didn't know him as well as me. Which he didn't.

"Sorry, yeah, of course." He shuffled his feet. "Are you looking for something? Can I help at all?" He peered into my locker. He wouldn't see much. I had nothing but school stuff in there, and one photo of me and my mom taken last Christmas.

"Why?" I shut the locker door with extra force, swinging my gear bag where it narrowly missed Jonah, and then staring up at him. I saw him wince, and I knew it was probably because I was rocking a full-on bitch face over why he kept popping up in my space.

And why did butterflies dance in my chest whenever I was near him?

"Why what?"

"You're always following me."

He winced. "I don't mean to, I'm just—"

"And then you're giving me food, and I just don't get it. What is up with that love thing?"

"Uhmm…" He was confused and took a step away from me.

"What do you have for me now?"

He was shifty, wouldn't quite meet my gaze. "Nothing."

I could tell he was lying, and that was frustrating. "Jonah?"

He bit his lip, then slipped off his backpack and reached inside, rummaging, the tip of his tongue poking out in concentration. Then, he smiled when he found what he was looking for and handed me my favorite cheesy Doritos. I took the bag from him, then waved it in front of me.

"How do you know these are my favorite?"

He dipped his gaze for a moment, then threw me a cautious smile. "You have them sometimes. Actually, a lot of times."

I didn't know what to say to that, and I wasn't even thinking about who I might meet in the corridor, just heading the way I'd normally go, Jonah catching up to me. I had stuff I wanted to say, things in my head that weren't making sense, like wanting to see Jonah smile, then wanting him to leave me alone. I was so sunk into my thoughts I never saw the group of boys after the turn on the corridor.

And that was when I walked right into Miles.

Chapter Seven

Jonah

I SHOULD HAVE SEEN HIM.

Somehow, I should have seen Miles and his new pack of cavemen before they rounded the corner outside the AP Chinese classroom. My spider sense should have tingled. Something. Anything. But nope, I was too obsessed with the way Tyler's pink hair curled at the ends to be aware of my surroundings. Which was unlike me. Being a photographer, I prided myself on being tuned into the world around me because that Pulitzer Prize-winning image could be anywhere.

Tyler hit the brakes with such speed that I ran up his back. Miles sneered down at him, then his gaze flew to me, and the sneer became a scowl.

"Looks like the queer boy has a secret admirer," Miles tossed out, which got a few guffaws from the other football players traveling with him. The four of them were a wall of muscle. "Is that it, Robinson? Are you letting the little fairy suck your dick?"

"Are you jealous?" Tyler flung up into his smirky face.

The fury that overtook Miles was both fascinating and terrifying all at once. It was like watching David Banner become Hulk. For a big guy, Miles was fast —must be the sprints the football players run— because he had his hand fisted and drawn back in a flash.

I heard someone shout as I moved around Tyler, shoving him into the AP Chinese classroom door as Miles' fist met my face. My knees buckled, blood spurted, people in the hall screamed, and the door behind us flew open.

Mass bedlam broke out around us as I fell to my ass, the pain exploding throughout my face. I'd been hit in the thigh with a line drive once when playing baseball with my friends at my old school. This felt like that, only to my face. It was pure hell. The hallway went fuzzy, black edges crept into my vision as my dress shirt and tie soaked up the blood.

"Jonah, oh my God!" Tyler cried out, or I think it was Tyler.

He sounded muzzy as I fought not to pass out while trying to sort out the tossed salad that was my thoughts. I blinked a few times, the shock setting in now, and saw tiny Ms. Chen in a flowery fall dress with a bronze belt taking on Miles. And the behemoth was backing down, his gridiron goons nowhere to be seen.

"Here, oh shit, we need to get you to the nurse," Tyler gasped as he placed a rolled-up wad of napkins to my face. I winced, the slight pressure of the paper to my nose making me feel sick to my stomach. "Sorry! Sorry, oh sorry!"

"M'kay," I said as Ms. Chen stood over me like a Doberman while the school security officer raced up to escort Miles away. I let my eyes close to combat the nausea because tossing my cookies on top of being a punching bag for a douche was not on my agenda for the day.

"Let me call for the nurse to bring a stretcher," Ms. Chen said after they led Miles off like the criminal that he was.

"No." I coughed, bloody spittle flying into the wad of napkins. "I… make… walk."

No way in hell were they carrying me on a

stretcher. I could take a punch. Robinson men were made of steel, my dad always said. Right then, I felt less like steel and more like wet pasta. I held the napkins to my face, gently, and allowed Tyler and Ms. Chen to help me to my feet. I was wobbly as hell, sickly, and coated in my blood. But Tyler looked fine. More than fine. Cute. Worried too, like super worried. I leaned into him more than Ms. Chen because I liked the way he felt next to me. His arm around my waist felt… right. I took about ten steps, then had to stop to throw up in a trash can outside the Spanish lab.

"Why is everyone lurking?" Ms. Chen was asking as Tyler patted my back while I coughed up everything in my belly. "Go on. Nothing more to see here."

The hallway emptied. I straightened, coughed, and wiped my mouth with my sleeve. Didn't seem to me that a little vomit on top of a few gallons of blood on my shirt would matter. Mom would birth a bison when she saw my shirt. Well, maybe not. Maybe she'd be proud of me for taking that haymaker to protect Tyler.

"Maybe you should sit down," Tyler was saying as I drifted back to the here and now. My face hurt like a mother. My nose throbbed steadily.

"Nope. Good." I wobbled my way to the nurse's

office, drawing wide-eyed stares from the teachers who were closing their doors to go home. Ms. Chen was mumbling to herself in Chinese as we rounded the corner of the language labs to find the sparkling new medical office at the end of a long hallway. A long, long hallway. Five hundred miles, at least. "Face hurts."

"We're almost there. I can call for a stretcher," Ms. Chen repeated.

I shook my head, then wished I hadn't. "Nope, Robinson men… steel," I lisped, then swallowed some blood. Gross.

Somehow, we made it inside the nurse's office. My legs chose then to let me down; thankfully, there was a cot behind me. Ms. Chen and Tyler guided me to the bed, then moved aside to let the nurse, a cool dude by the name of Mr. Wright—no relation to the famous flying Wright Brothers, he liked to say—bustle in to tend to me, while Tyler was taken out of the room by Ms. Chen. My face hurt so badly I wanted to cry. Mr. Wright was a young guy, an LPN, who had joined the Chesterford staff last year right out of nursing school. A gangly redhead with a soothing aura, he asked me a lot of questions about silly things like the date, who was president, and where we were, while having me pinch my lower nose shut. I answered the way he wanted, I guess.

"Just like to check you don't have a concussion. Now lean forward, not back. Blood will irritate your stomach and make you sick." He eased me forward.

"Already puked," I mumbled.

"Yuck. That's the worst. You can close your eyes. Try focusing on your breathing. Slow, steady, in and out." After a few moments, he had me sit back slowly, studied my face, and shone a tiny light into my eyes before applying an ice bag to the bridge of my nose. "Whoever clocked you did a bang-up job." He tenderly touched my face. I hissed. "Sorry. I don't think its broken, but you're going to have some nice shiners for Thanksgiving. You should see your primary care provider anyway in case there is a need to realign. Your file states your parents are fine with you getting OTC pain relief, so let's get a few of those into you."

Oh shit. My folks were going to freak the hell out. Doctor bills we did not need. Stupid fucking Miles. I groaned. Mr. Wright ran off to get me some ibuprofen and a glass of water. I swallowed the tablets down. The room was dim, the lights low, and my head was pounding. I toed off my shoes and lay down now that the bleeding was done. I could hear the nurse talking to someone, a man, probably the assistant principal or even the principal. Breathing through my nose was impossible now, as both sides had clots in them. My mouth tasted like old blood. A headache the size of a mountain was starting behind my eyes. Oh, and my gut was still bubbling like a witch's cauldron. But Tyler was okay. That was the important thing. Miles was done pushing my… *shit*…he's not *my* anything.

I must have drifted off—how I had no clue—because the door opening and my mother rushing in startled me.

"Oh, Jonah," she gasped as the nurse and the principal entered behind her. She flew over to my cot, sat down beside me, and cried soft tears as she looked at my face. My eyes were puffy now, swollen and, more than likely, already turning purple. "Honey, what on earth happened?"

She helped me sit up. I felt like shit and told her so. She wiped at her cheeks, then patted my shoulder. Mom handed me the ice bag, which I placed on my face as she rubbed small circles on my back.

"Jonah, can you tell us what happened?" Principal Foster asked, hovering behind the nurse. I'd met Principal Foster when I first came here. There had been some sort of PR thing where I'd posed in my new uniform, smiling, while shaking hands with the principal. He was an older White guy with snowy hair and dark-framed glasses.

I relayed what had taken place. Mom rubbed my back harder when I repeated what had been said to me and Tyler right before Tyler had fired back at Miles. Then, the punch had come. After that, things were kind of hazy.

Principal Foster looked pissed. "It's unforgiveable that you were hurt on school grounds. Mr. Brooks and the other young men who were with him are in my office awaiting their parents. We'll deal with them appropriately, make no mistake. We do not allow fighting on school grounds, nor do we condone verbal attacks based on race, gender, or sexuality. I wish this issue had been brought to our attention before it escalated, but now that the school knows, it will be dealt with swiftly. Mrs. Robinson, please take Jonah home. He's excused for the rest of the week to recover. If he needs to be out next week, we will require a doctor's note. Again, on behalf of the staff and management of Chesterford Academy, you have my deepest apologies."

Mom said nothing. I mumbled a thanks. Principal Foster hustled out, his back stiff, his gait purposeful. I hoped he laid into Miles big time.

"Well, at least they have the incident recorded and

several dozen witnesses," Mom whispered while trying to help me into a bulky sweater she had brought from home. It was my favorite one, a thick blue cardigan my grandmother had knitted for me before she passed away. It had a few holes here and there, but it was my sick sweater. And man, was I feeling sick all over. Every inch of me ached. "They won't be able to blame it on the Black boy this time."

"Mom, I did the things the school blamed on me," I tried to get out, but my words were garbled. I'd done the crime with Tyler, and I'd deserved the time, or suspension, or whatever. I knew she was probably referring to the wider picture, but I felt compelled to say something.

For what it was worth.

Nurse Wright made a sound in the corner while filling out forms. I eased my arm into the right sleeve, then the left, then tenderly got to my feet. The room didn't spin this time, and my stomach didn't heave, so that was good. If I never threw up in front of half the student body again, that would be awesome. Nothing says cool dude like a man with his head in a trash can making sounds like a cat coughing up a hairball.

Mom signed me out, and we trudged down the silent halls. We stopped at my locker. My eyes were so swollen that I couldn't see the lock well, so Mom had to enter the combination. Once we had my books and my coat, she walked me outside. The cold air smacked me in the face with the force of a right hook from Miles the Meathead.

"We're parked in front," Mom said gently, toting my backpack and my books. I felt like hammered shit, to quote my father. "We're going to the walk-in clinic to get some X-rays of your nose."

"It's fine," I replied as I huffed icy cold air into my lungs. I hated breathing through my mouth. "Give me… character," I added to, hopefully, stop her from spending more cash on my face. If it was broken and crooked, who cared? Chicks and dudes dig scars and busted noses. "I'll tell people… I was in a bar fight."

She snorted sadly. Someone called my name. I glanced to the left to see Tyler racing at me, fully geared for hockey aside from his skates, with my camera in his hand. How had I not noticed it was missing?!

"Hey, oh man, you look like you got punched by Adler Lockhart," Tyler whispered as he skidded to a halt on the frosty sidewalk. "Emily Lynch had it. She picked it up in the hallway after Miles hit you. She gave it to me because…" He scratched at his head, mussing up his bright pink hair. "I don't know why.

She thought we were friends since you took that punch for me. Why did you *do* that?"

Mom took my camera before looking from Tyler to me. I shrugged. "I didn't want him to hit you, I guess."

My mother pressed a tiny kiss to my hair. Tyler stared at me as if I were a troll that had just recited *Hamlet*. I totally felt like a troll right now. My face had to be frightening as hell.

"Thanks," Tyler said softly, his expression murky with confusion. "If there's anything that I can do to pay you back just—"

"Come visit me?"

Tyler's green eyes flared. "You mean like at home?"

"Yeah, please. I don't really have any other friends."

Tyler stared openly.

"We better get you to the clinic. Tyler, thank you for looking out for Jonah's camera while he was incapacitated. And please, come visit him while he rests up from the attack." She gave Tyler a warm, but oh-so weary smile.

Mom steered me to our car, opening the door for me, then tucking me into the passenger seat as if I were Polly's age or something. Not going to lie, her fussing felt good. Tyler stood on the sidewalk, wind blowing his bubblegum hair as the naked trees on the quad shook and shuddered, watching me trying to watch him. My vision was now nothing more than slits. When the car started, Tyler raised a hand. I did the same.

Mom pulled away from the school. I let my head fall back to the rest, sighed, and prayed Tyler would drop by while I was home, even though I was sure he wouldn't.

Chapter Eight

Tyler

"Mr. Corrigan?"

I didn't have to turn to know that Principal Foster was right behind me—no one else called me Mr. *anything* in quite the same way, and it was usually before he explained boys had a lot of energy and that, maybe, if I didn't have pink hair and *everything else,* I might not have been a target for the more *boisterous* kids. I can't say he excused everything and left me hanging—there was always a punishment for anyone caught intimidating me or others—but there was always the warning that the only way to stay safe was to maybe, *possibly if I wanted* to, conform.

He was all talk about no fights on school grounds

and apologizing to my mom about something that happened to me, but after that, it was always that casual warning to keep my head down. I didn't know if he was being sympathetic or not.

"Tyler?" he asked, and this time, stuck to just my first name.

There was no point in me heading to hockey practice now. I'd missed the start of it, and when the news hit about what happened, I doubted the coach would hassle me for it. I'd hung around, watching from afar, hating what happened to Jonah, and regretting getting even a hint of a backbone where Jonah was concerned. Look where it got me.

Look where it got Jonah.

I turned to face the principal. "Sir," I responded, calm, collected, and waiting for the advice. I'd been waiting since for the incident to be connected to me, and to have to listen to the advice that the principal liked to dispense.

"Could we talk?" He didn't look all bluster like he usually did. If anything, he seemed nervous. "In my office? Your mom is on her way here."

My heart sank. Why did he call my mom when I wasn't the one at the end of the fist? Nope, that had been poor Jonah with the split face and the blood.

"Why?" I blurted, and he winced. "Never mind." I

strode after him, and we took a left, then a right, and went straight into the office where I'd been more than a few times over the past year. It was a room full of hopelessness, and what made it worse was that the principal didn't sit behind his desk.

"I want to apologize for what happened in my school," he said, and gestured for me to sit. "It's no excuse, but I didn't realize just how far this had gone with Miles to take it out on someone I thought was his friend."

"Jonah and Miles aren't friends," I offered quickly, and he did that whole wince thing again.

Mom slammed open the door. "Tyler!" She went straight to my side, cupping my chin and scrutinizing me.

"I'm okay, Mom. It wasn't me who got hit."

"Who hit who?" someone else asked, and I peered past my mom to see Jim, Felix's dad, and wondered why he and my mom were here together, and then...

Oh shit. Really? Was Jim *freaking* Maxwell-Sinclair pulling the dad card just because he was dating my mom? I never wanted the dad I had, let alone a replacement one. Close behind him was Felix, his face like thunder, Soren right next to him.

"What did Jonah do?" Felix snapped and attempted to dart around his dad, but Soren used all his hockey blocking moves to keep him out of the room.

It was chaos, and I stood sharply and waved my hands in front of me, then pointed at Felix first. "Jonah did nothing apart from take the hit that was supposed to be for me, so go away." He didn't move, so I turned to Soren. "Take him away."

Soren nodded and tugged Felix hard out of the doorway. Felix shot me angry glances as he stumble-walked away with his boyfriend. One down…

Then it was Principal Foster's turn to hear what I really thought. "I don't need apologies from you or the school. You have a rule saying there's to be no bullying and everything should be sunshine and rainbows, but that isn't real life. Something needs fixing." I inhaled and winced inwardly, but the principal was quiet and chagrined, and not at all giving me a lifetime of detention.

And next I turned to my mom and her… her whatever… "I don't need you here, Mom. I love you, and I'm happy you came to find out how I am, but I'm grown up and I can handle this on my own."

She made to say something, then hugged me, and I returned the hug with emotion.

Finally, it was Felix's dad's turn. "You're good for

my mom, Mr. Maxwell-Sinclair. I get that, but I don't need a new dad. Okay?"

"I'm sorry," Jim apologized immediately and looked stricken, and there went my guilt button again.

"I need to go visit Jonah and thank him for getting in the way of Miles' fist."

Principal Foster nodded, Jim copied him, and Mom gave me one of her thoughtful, loving smiles that meant we'd be talking more on all of this later.

But for now, I had one place I wanted to be. Checking on Jonah.

I left the office at a run, realizing, belatedly, that I didn't know where Jonah lived, then hunted down Felix, hoping he and Soren hadn't left like the rest of the kids, as the day was well over now. As soon as Soren saw me heading their way, he shoved Felix front and center. "Do it," he demanded.

"I'm really sorry," Felix said. "I don't mean to make you think that... I don't think that you... shit..."

"He knows you can look after yourself; he's just a possessive, overprotective, guilt-ridden prick," Soren finished on a sigh.

I waited for him and Felix to tussle after that, but all Felix did was nod with an unhappy expression.

"What he said," he finally broke the awkward silence.

I didn't have time for this. I needed to see Jonah. "Okay then."

"So, I'll try not to do it again, but if Miles… if he…"

"Yeah," I said, and that seemed to be enough. "Anyway, I need Jonah's address if I'm going to check on him."

"Grandpa can take you," Soren suggested. "He's picking me up."

"Thank you," I said, and waited for Soren to ask. I saw his grandpa nod, and Soren gestured me over. Only, as soon as I got near the car, I pointed at the front door. "Shotgun to navigate," I said, and dared Felix to argue.

Seemed as if, today, I could get away with anything because he didn't offer me a single peep, not that he would, because then he and Soren got to share the back seat. Soren's grandpa was a sweet guy who wanted to talk about bacon, which I liked because I didn't want to talk about hockey, although Soren and Felix were dissecting our last game to death.

"And that's why I like the maple syrup on those," Soren's grandpa summarized.

I nodded along. "Same," I lied—I hadn't been listening as well as I should have.

When we arrived at the house, Soren immediately spoke up. "We'll wait out here," he suggested, but I shook my head.

"Mom is on call; she'll pick me up. Thank you," I added to Soren's grandpa, who nodded and smiled.

"Remember the maple syrup," he said.

"I will, sir."

"But if you're just saying hi, we can wait," Felix interrupted the bacon chat from the back seat, and I met his gaze in the mirror. He subsided quickly.

"I might be here hours," I said, then repeated it for good measure. "Hours!"

No one argued, and I smiled back at Soren. "Thanks for organizing the ride."

"Always," he said with a smile, and I caught the quick kiss that Felix gave Soren as Soren moved to sit up front with his grandpa. I don't know how to explain it, but my heart smiled to see them so happy together. I wanted that. I wanted to feel like my heart was smiling, with casual kisses, and I-love-yous, and hugs, and stupid little shared stories.

I waited at the door for a second, made sure they drove away, even sketched a little wave at them when Felix waved. Idiot. Then, I couldn't put off going inside, so I knocked. The house itself was an older model, set back from the road; the yard was coated with frost and there were glimpses of toys in the flowers—a Barbie here, a teacup there, the handlebars and front wheel of a bike poking around the corner—and I seemed to recall from a family day that Jonah had sisters? No one was answering, but then the door opened on the chain.

"Yes?" a little voice asked, and my gaze traveled down until I met wide and curious eyes and went to a half crouch. Given how short I was, this must be a very little sister.

"Hi. I'm Tyler, Jonah's uhm… friend. Can I see him?"

"He has an ouchie," the little girl informed me.

I nodded. "I know."

"He cried."

Great. Now my smiley heart was all twisted up and compassionate and sad, and I really needed to see Jonah to find out what he'd been thinking. Then to ask him about why he didn't have friends, and find out about his family, and his house, and his neighborhood.

"I bet he did," I said. "Can you get your mom, or your dad?"

She peered out at me, and for a few moments, we

stared in silence, then she slammed the door shut, or as hard as a small kid could. Odds were bad that she even came back, and I told myself I'd give it a minute before I knocked again. Or maybe I could find Jonah's room and throw rocks at his window.

The door chain rattled and, this time, the door opened wide—this must be Jonah's dad, because there was no sign of recognition until he clocked my uniform.

"Emma!" he bellowed. "Someone's here!"

Jonah's mom appeared at his side; her arms full of the same small girl I'd already spoken to.

"Tyler, hello." She was cautious, the little girl grimaced, and Jonah's dad glared at me. It was the unholy trinity of welcomes.

"Uhm…" Shoulders back, tilt chin up. "Jonah said I could visit, so I thought, strike while the iron's hot and all that."

Jonah's dad sniffed and cast his gaze from my head to my toes. Great. He was seeing the pink hair, and the badges on the messenger bag over my shoulder, and I just knew what he was thinking. I tilted my chin a lot more and met his judgmental gaze steadily.

"You one of those kids who hurt my son?!" he demanded.

Jonah's mom hushed him. "No, this is the one who Jonah was protecting," she faux-whispered.

His stern, disapproving demeanor melted away in an instant, and he opened the door and gestured me inside. "Come in, come in. Welcome to our home. I'm Terrence, and this is my wife Emma, and this here is Polly, our youngest. Say hi, Polly."

"Hi," Polly dutifully recited, then wriggled her way down from her mom's hold and vanished into the bowels of the house.

"We met today," Emma said, then grasped my upper arms and peered at me as if she was checking me for damage. She had the clearest blue eyes, and they were brimming with worry. "Are you okay?"

"Yes, I'm fine, it was Jonah who…"

She released her hold and patted my arm. "Good."

"I haven't brought anything, like grapes or whatever." Maybe I should have asked Soren's grandpa to stop at a gas station for flowers, or chocolate, or a teddy, or something that said, thank you for taking a punch meant for me after I confronted the school bully and caused him to go nuclear.

"He's feeling sorry for himself, and I'm not sure grapes would help," his mom said, then tugged her husband to one side and gestured at the stairs. "First door on the left, the one with the *Fortnite* poster. I'll bring up some snacks and drinks soon."

"Thank you, I don't want to be a bother."

"It's been a long time since Jonah had friends over," she said and exchanged glances with her husband, who pulled her into a sideways hug. "Anyway." Her smile brightened. "Go on up and see Grumpy McGrumpy."

I slipped off my bag, and she took it and my jacket from me and added it to the pile of stuff hanging on the newel post at the bottom of the stairs, smoothing it flat. She didn't comment on the badges or stare at me weirdly. If anything, Jonah's parents were cool as hell. Kind of like my mom, really. I stopped at the top of the stairs, sent a quick *love you* to my mom, adding to the earlier message where I'd explained I was visiting Jonah. I knew she and I needed to talk about what I'd said to the principal, and about Dad, and God, so many things. She sent me a message back, just as quick, to say she loved me too, and that she'd sent me some money to order pizza when I got home.

I smiled at that—seemed as if food was the story of our family, as well as Jonah's.

Taking a breath, I knocked on the door.

"No, I don't want to play tea parties, Polly!" a

nasally voice that sounded completely unlike Jonah came from inside.

"It's not Polly, it's… uhm… me," I said.

I heard some banging, crashing, and scurrying, and then, after a wait of at least a minute during which I stared at the poster of Deadfire on his door, admiring the beautiful lines of the artwork, Jonah cracked open his door, much as his sister had done. Then, he opened his wider and stepped back.

Shit, he was a mess.

"Shit," I said, then placed a hand over my mouth, remembering belatedly that his little sister might lurk somewhere close by.

"How bad is it?" Jonah asked mournfully.

"Super bad, like all…" I waved a hand at my face, "blotchy and cut, and there's blood there."

He went cross-eyed trying to check out his nose, which was cute and stupid. Then, he laughed, not a big belly laugh, but a soft, almost shy sound that made my chest tight.

"It's not broken, but I think my modeling days are over," he said after a moment and smiled, but then winced before shuffling back even more. "You want to come in?"

I stepped inside, took in a tidy space—small, but perfectly formed—then stood, not sure what to say or do. I saw a plate of rice and chicken. "Am I interrupting dinner?" I asked. Doh. Of course, I was.

"I couldn't manage it," he said ruefully and nudged it to one side. "Not hungry anyway." He left the door open. "Rules, when I have people over," he explained.

"Even when it's a boy?" I asked with a smile, and wished I hadn't when he raised an eyebrow, then winced.

"Yep," he said, and my chest tightened at the thought of other boys coming over which forced an open door policy. I massaged the ache as he explained. "Mom and Dad are all equality rules in this house. No boys or girls over with a shut door until I either marry or leave home. Dad's words, not mine." He laughed then, and groaned because it must have hurt. He patted a chair at a small desk, which I sat on, then he took the bed, cross-legged, and stared at me. Where had that flash of jealousy come from? Why was I thinking about Jonah with another boy and feeling so wrong about it all.

I met his steady gaze, and the jealousy became guilt about his face, and the punch, and that I was the one who'd wound up Miles.

"Fuck, Jonah. I'm so sorry."

Chapter Nine

Jonah

I DID MY BEST TO GIVE TYLER A LOOK THAT SAID there was nothing for him to be sorry about, but given my face was probably like Glass Joe after Mike Tyson whaled on him in that old Nintendo game, the eye roll kind of lost its meaning.

"Dude, seriously, you have nothing to be sorry about. I should be the one apologizing to you for being a huge scrotum."

He shoved a shank of pink hair from his eyes. It was a motion that made him seem really vulnerable and really cute all at once.

"It's cool. You were in your scrotum era."

"Totally. So don't feel bad. I don't." He arched a

thin eyebrow. "Well, okay, I feel bad physically, but mentally I feel way better than I have in forever. Like…" I pulled in a breath, then glanced around the room at my posters. At the famous Black photographers' collage on my closet door to a random corkboard with ticket stubs, shots of the fam, and papers that I'd done well on or totally aced. "I've never really fit in anywhere. It's been worse since I started attending Chesterford, but even back in my old school, I was too Black for the White kids and too White for the Black kids. Then I started… you know." I squinted down at the bi bracelet on my wrist and gave it a snap. His eyes rounded in surprise. "Then I kind of started struggling with this, too."

Tyler glanced over his shoulder. The hall was empty and quiet. Something that didn't happen often in our house. The parental units must have slipped in a Disney movie. That was the only thing that kept the girls quiet for any length of time.

"You're bi?" he asked on a whisper.

I shrugged. "I think so, maybe. Like…" I fiddled with the rubber bracelet as I stared down at my feet. "There've been a few famous guys that I've thought I would totally date, you know, and maybe more with, but that was just famous guys. Who doesn't think that Algee Smith is kissable?"

"No one," Tyler concurred, which made me feel less weird about telling him all of this.

Was I coming out to Tyler? Man, that was heavy. Yet, it didn't feel heavy at all. It felt right.

"So yeah, those were famous guys, right?" I moved next to him so we could keep the conversation on the DL. Lana was sneaky as hell when she wanted to be. The other two were too young to really be covert, but Lana was super ninja when she wanted to be. Tyler scooted over a bit, his feet on the rather worn carpeting right beside mine. Mine were bigger by a lot. "Then, I came to Chesterford and…"

"Hey, you don't have to tell me if you're crushing on someone in school. That's totally something you can keep locked down tight." He gave my ankle a tiny nudge with his foot. "Seriously, I have like a dozen crushes per semester. We have some gorgeous people at Chesterford."

I snuck a peek to the side. Tyler was smiling softly, his gaze on the poster of Johny Pitts on the ceiling.

"Yeah, we have some gorgeous people," I whispered, then quickly glanced back down at our feet. "Anyway, so I have this two-bi-is-too-bad thing happening."

"Two bi?"

"Yeah, biracial and bisexual, and it's really fucking hard." I exhaled through my nose, but the air leaked out. The wheezy breath sounded stupid as shit. I snorted, which hurt, but not as badly as it hurt just an hour ago. Maybe it was the meds and ice, or maybe it was Tyler making the pain lessen. "Not being accepted for who you are sucks."

"I know how that feels." That pulled my focus from our differently sized feet. "I mean, I totally get what it feels like to be the odd dude out. I'm femme, right?" I nodded because I didn't want to box him into a term that maybe he wasn't happy with. "Right, and I embrace that about myself. I can be a femme male and still play hockey, or at least I think so. Shame the rest of the world is all up in arms if I wear eyeliner or nail polish to a game."

"That sucks," I replied because it did. "Why does stupid shit matter to so many people? Guys can wear makeup. Girls can wear a tie and a vest. Those outdated gender norm clothes rules are stupid. I mean, I'm not feeling the eyeliner, but my sisters paint my toes all the time. Check it." I reached down, removed my socks, and wiggled my bright pink toenails.

Tyler chuckled, then tore off his socks to show me his purple glitter toenails. We both grinned at our pedicures, then at each other. Well, I tried to grin.

Smiling with two shiners and a puffy nose was hard and made my eyes water, but it was worth it to see Tyler being so happy and chill. He was always so tense at school. "And this is nothing. A week ago, I was in a tutu serving tea to three ninja princesses."

"I bet you looked adorable," he said, then lowered his foot. His pinkie toe brushed my pinkie toe. A sizzling jolt of awareness raced up my calf, through my thigh, and right to my groin. Not wanting to act like a toe slut, but really wanting more, I wiggled my foot over a few inches. I glanced to the side. His eyes met mine. He curled his toes, then stretched them out, his little toe slipping under my little toe, and there it stayed.

We were holding toes.

I wasn't sure if that was anywhere near the same as holding hands. Maybe pinkie toe-holding was a funny thing two dudes did, but I suspected not. Miles had never let any part of his body touch mine, or any other guys, unless he was on the football field. Off the turf, two guys touching was *fag behavior*, but on the field, two guys could slap each other's asses, and that was *totally cool and macho*.

"I hope you know you can talk to me about feeling different," Tyler said, yanking me back from contemplating sports and masculinity. I nodded, my gaze flicking to him as he spoke. He needed to sweep back that strand of pink hair again. I wanted to tuck it behind his ear so badly, but that might be too creepy, so I sat on my hands and contented myself with toe-holding. "We're in the same boat, even though our storms are a little different. Also, just so you know, the Chesterford GSA is full of really cool students, all queer in one glorious form or another, so if you wanted to join us, you'd just be Jonah, the guy who takes all those amazing shots for the school paper."

"You think they're amazing?" I asked.

"Yeah, especially the ones with me," he teased, then giggle-snorted.

"Those are my faves," I confessed softly and got a look that might have set the sheets on fire if Polly hadn't chosen that moment to come bouncing in with a book. We both yanked our feet apart, leaving my little toe really sad and lonely.

"I did eat dinner! Jo-bah is bed time," she announced as she climbed between Tyler and me, her pajama leggings up over her knees and one slipper missing. "Jo-bah read." She shoved the book into my chest, then stared up at Tyler while tugging on a tight curly pigtail. "Jo-bah ouch face is sad."

I glanced at Tyler. "Sorry, I kind of read to her most nights."

"Sorry, oh gosh, sorry, boys." Mom announced as she rushed in with a basket of clothes under one arm and a box of graham crackers in her other hand. "She was supposed to wait for me to fold the laundry before her story tonight." Mom placed the basket on the floor, dug out two bottles of apple juice, passed them to Tyler and me, then reached for my baby sister. Polly was having none of it. She began to wail and kick.

"She's okay. Really, we'll read the book, then she can go to bed," I said, easing my sister from my mother. Polly burrowed into my chest, her thumb now in her mouth, and lay her head on my chest.

"I should go," Tyler said, bending down to find his socks.

"No, you can stay. I mean if you want to listen to me read *Piggies on Parade*," I hurried to say—hopeful that he would stay, but sure he wouldn't. I mean, who wants to sit around and listen to a kid's book being read by someone who sounded like they had cotton batting in their sinuses?

"Sure, yeah, okay," he said a moment later, pulling on his socks, then whispering a shy thanks to my mom for the tiny bottle of juice and box of dollar store graham crackers. "I've never read that one."

"Piggies parade," Polly mumbled. I smiled down

at her, then over at Tyler. He smiled back. My mom smiled down at us. So much smiling was taking place. "Jo-bah, read!"

"Sorry, your highness," I replied as my mom left us to the story of four piggies planning a parade for Pride. Inclusivity was big around here, which was good because I suspected I'd be having a big sit-down with the folks soon about their only son wanting to date boys. Or one boy in particular…

I GOT THREE DAYS OFF TO RECOVER FROM THE PUNCH in the face.

During that time, Tyler came over three times— twice alone, and once with Soren. Felix was noticeably absent on that third visit, and Soren did his best to not talk too much about his boyfriend, which I appreciated, but wasn't necessary. Felix and I would sort shit out in our own time. We would have to eventually. It would get super uncomfortable to be on a school bus with the team riding all over the state with that enormous dark cloud still floating over our heads.

Even with the elephant in the room, Tyler, Soren, and I had a good time that night. Soren was a streamer and an avid gamer, so we'd spent several hours sitting on the floor of my room playing *Minecraft*. We built a massive village that we could all access and work on when we were home. It felt good to add Tyler and Soren to my friends on the server.

Also, it was funny how stepping up had made me into something popular. Seemed a lot of kids in school had found that heroic. My friend requests and follows were climbing. Quite a few were the Coyotes, sure, but about thirty had been kids I barely knew. Tyler had pointed out that several were from the GSA, but many others were just good kids who stood behind me standing up to Miles.

My first day back, Tyler met me at the front doors, Soren, and a pouting Felix with him, and we made our way into the hallowed halls. Several girls called greetings, and a few guys nodded at me, one flashing a peace sign.

"That's Rudy," Tyler explained as we hustled to first period. "He's the president of the GSA, if you'd like to talk to him about maybe joining," he said on the sly.

Soren and Felix, behind us, talked to a few of the Coyotes, who were lingering outside the history classrooms.

"I'd rather talk to you," I confessed. He glanced

up at me, his face cloudy, the expression hard to read. "About joining."

"Oh, yeah, sure. Just let me know when you think you're ready. I'll be there." He smiled at me. The apple-cinnamon oatmeal I'd made for me and the girls while Mom and Dad had eggs with scrapple— gross stuff that scrapple—did a flip-flop. I burped silently, gave Tyler a bob of my head, then raced off to English for first period.

The day went... incredibly well. I saw no sign of Miles. He was still in school as far as the news network went. There was a hearing he had to attend before he could be suspended, but wherever he was, he was not in my line of sight. Maybe he was keeping his distance. I hoped so. Even at lunch, there were no sightings. I sat with the team, Tyler sitting beside me, and while I didn't talk much, the guys were much warmer. Felix was touchy, shooting looks my way, then jerking his sight away when I glanced up, but that was okay. Not great, but I could handle it.

Thanksgiving break started next Wednesday and ran through the following Monday, and I had fallen behind on my newspaper work. Mr. Wheeler met me in the *Chronicle* office after last class, and we spent about an hour sorting through my pictures and downloading them to the paper's computer. Mom was working a later shift, so Dad would swing by to pick me up after he was done at work. With an hour or so to kill, I opted to visit the school library to do my homework. It was quieter at the library than it was at home.

The halls were empty now, my footfalls bouncing off the tiled floors, as I made my way to my locker. The janitorial staff were now at work, cleaning the classrooms, mopping the floors, scouring the bathrooms. I rounded a corner by the teachers' lounge, saw the bright yellow wet floor sign propped up in the corridor, and slowly made my way down the hall to my locker.

"Hey there, Jonah," a grizzled voice called.

I paused, turned, and saw old Desmond Parks exiting the teachers' lounge with a small blue tote of cleaning supplies. He was wearing coveralls with some bleach spots and old sneakers. I'd taken some shots of him for a project that Soren and Felix had been working on, but the fact that he remembered my name was surprising.

"Yes, sir?" I asked, taking care to not move as I assumed he was going to bitch at me for walking on his freshly mopped floor.

He padded over the wet tiles, his sneakers squeaking. Guess he wasn't worried about the mop job. I met his gaze as he neared the cart, then placed his tote atop it.

"Glad to see that you finally yanked your head out of your ass," he remarked, the overhead lights highlighting the silver strands in his closely cropped hair.

"Sorry?" I asked after I found my tongue. What kind of right did this old Black dude have to talk to me like I was a jerk. I mean, I was—or had been—but who was he to call me out?

"You heard me," he replied, turning to look right into my soul. "You're a smart young man. Got a scholarship to this school for your photography. Yeah, I know about you. I like to keep an eye on the kids of color that come through this school. Most are good, but you, well, you were a rotten egg for a while."

Oh. Okay, well, yeah, I sort of was at that. "I'm not that way anymore."

"That remains to be seen." He dug into the front pocket of his overalls for a stick of gum as he talked. "You did a good thing the other day sticking up for that boy with the pink hair." He unwrapped the light green stick of spearmint, folded it in half, then put it into his mouth. "I can't rightfully say why a boy wants to have pink hair, but just because I don't understand it, don't mean he shouldn't be able to have his hair the color that makes him happy."

"Yeah," I mumbled, unsure of where this was going other than Desmond calling me an asshole. Previous asshole.

"So, you taking that shot says a lot about your character. Ditching that moron Miles was another. I never understood why you would take up with a racist jerk like that boy, but then again, lots of people of all colors do stupid things. Thankfully, you wised up and kicked his ass to the curb like the bag of trash he is, and trust me, I know trash."

"Yes, sir," I said wishing this little pep talk, or whatever it was, would wrap up. I didn't *really* like being reminded of my jerkoff status.

"You got a real chance here, Jonah. I wish I'd have had the opportunities that you young kids have now. Don't screw things up. Keep your head on straight, pick good friends, listen to your parents, and be smart. Go to college, take pictures, and find fame. You got the talent." He poked me with a calloused finger. "Do not go back to being a stooge for some gorilla. You need to represent for all the other kids with darker skin that are going to come along after you graduate. Make a legacy to be proud of, Jonah."

"Yes, sir, I will," I whispered, feeling small as hell

for being called out by a janitor. I mean, seriously, this guy was two years away from going off to war when he was my age, and here I was—or had been— throwing away a chance he would have died for back in the sixties. "I promise."

"Good. Now get your books and stop tracking up my clean hallway." He waved me off, then entered the next room to empty trash cans and slop a mop over the dirt dozens of designer shoes tracked in on the daily.

I hurried off, head filled with thoughts that swirled around like a tornado. It was shocking and humbling to see just how many people paid attention to what choices you made in life. I hoped the decisions I was making now would be the proper ones to make Desmond proud.

Chapter Ten

Tyler

JONAH: *FAM AFTER EATING BODYWEIGHT IN TURKEY and pie #ThanksgivingVibes #fat #sleepy #football*

I opened the photo to see Jonah laid out on the sofa, all three of his sisters in on the selfie, his mom grinning, and his dad pretend-pouting. It was the perfect snapshot of an awesome family, and one I'd gotten to know a little over the past couple of weeks.

Tyler: *Say hi to everyone*

When Jonah had come back to school, it was awkward between us at first—a lot of gossipy kids and pointing fingers. He'd been uncomfortable with the attention and the weight of all the questions and seemed to avoid me. I'd like to say that we'd connected after the punch, but we didn't immediately gravitate together, at first, we were on opposite ends of the hockey table in the cafeteria, but subtly, day by day, we moved nearer, and by the end of the first week, we were on the end, opposite each other, and then there was even more awkward.

Visiting him at home had been easy, but here in school, there was this *thing* growing between us that was under so much scrutiny it was impossible to talk about anything that wasn't hockey or school.

That had been when the messaging started, when we realized it was easier to message each other instead of learning about who we were face-to-face. We were friends, and I could ask him anything I wanted when he wasn't right there in front of me.

Maybe it was because I didn't want him to see that I went hot whenever he talked to me, or that my belly was full of butterflies every moment I thought about him.

But I didn't have a happy Thanksgiving selfie to send back to him because my Thanksgiving dinner was a strained, awkward, miserable, mess, and I was thinking it was all my fault. Mom had been so excited when Jim had invited us over to his and Felix's new place for Thanksgiving, but it had all gone wrong from the moment the door opened. The naive part of me had hoped this could have been the first family Thanksgiving I'd ever enjoyed.

Of course, we had the day when Dad was around, but it was never any kind of family thing, more an excuse for my dad to drink and end up hitting my mom and…

I can't go there.

I'd arrived at the house, hefting two pies my mom had been up early to make. My eyeliner was on point, lips glossy, hair styled, and I was wearing my favorite shirt, tie-dyed in all colors of the rainbow. I felt pretty and confident and I was sure that this was going to be the best day—the day that me, Mom, Jim, and Felix had fun.

That fizzing feeling of hope was vanquished as soon as Felix opened the door and wouldn't look at me. His restrained hello to Mom was about the worst kind of start, and it had gone downhill from there.

"Missing Soren?" I teased him—anything to get a smile—but he frowned.

"We're not joined at the hip," he muttered, then slunk away through a door I supposed must lead to a kitchen. I hadn't visited this new house of theirs before. It wasn't far from their old place, but about a fifth of the size, but when the door opened the scent of turkey hit me, so yeah, Felix had gone to hide in the kitchen. The aroma of roasted turkey was glorious, but the taste of Felix's running away was bitter.

Jim came out through the same door, wearing an apron with the James Bond gunshot logo and the words *License to Grill*. It was such a dad apron that it made me smile.

It was so normal. *Maybe this will be okay.*

"Guys! You made it!"

Next to me, Mom was a mess of smiles, and her expression was incandescent with happy when Jim pulled her into a hug. He didn't quite know what to do with me, but it was okay—I had pie in my hands, which made things less awkward because it made hugging or shaking hands impossible. He pressed a hand to my shoulder instead and squeezed briefly.

I was cool with that.

"Come through, this is the dining room, and through there is the kitchen. Can I get you a drink? Do you want me to take the pies?"

"I can carry them through," I said.

He nodded, slipping his arm over my mom's shoulder, and giving her another hug, this time, a cute kissy kind of hug. I loved him for how he made my mom laugh, and how she gave a genuine smile whenever they were together.

That was the high point. The only good bit really.

Because once we were at the table, me kitty-corner to Felix, it was shit, even when Jim tried to get us to relax.

Hell, he was trying so hard.

"So, Felix said you broke the school record for skating a lap," Jim encouraged, after exhausting movies, school, and the weather. He probably thought hockey was a safe subject, but not even that got Felix to talk. If anything, Felix went quieter as he picked at his dinner and avoided looking at me.

Mom was using that high-pitched laugh of hers, the one that sounded forced, trying to be bright and fun and over-the-top vivacious. Jim was clearly nervous, but he was also forcing jollity, raising his glass in a toast at the drop of the hat. "*Here's to friends. Here's to family. Here's to mashed potatoes.*" I could feel the worry in both him and my mom, the way Felix wasn't joining in, and I didn't know how to fix things. It was clear that Mom had fallen for Jim, and that they were happy together, after all, I'd just seen them in the kitchen, laughing and hugging as she cut up pie. They didn't know I'd seen them, and I backed out right away, hands still full of condiments, straight into Felix, who apologized, sidestepped me, and then scampered back to the table in double time.

This was ridiculous. Even more so when Jim and Mom came back out and placed the slices on the table along with a shit ton of other sweet treats, one at a time.

"Your mom said you like chocolate, right?" he said. "So, I got a cheesecake, some of those nutty bar things, banoffee pie, which isn't strictly chocolate, but it has all the shavings on top. And of course, pumpkin pie. Hmmm. What else…" He peered at the enormous collection of diabetes-inducing candy-based desserts he'd laid out. "Oh, and I have three kinds of chocolate sprinkles, not that you have to have them, but Felix likes them, and I thought you might… not that I'm assuming what you like… or assuming…" He sat down after running out of things to say, and everyone was silent.

"Okay," I said, and Mom glanced at me, because that was not a kind *okay,* it was an okay filled with warning. "Mr. Maxwell-Sinclair?"

"You can call me Jim," he said immediately.

"Jim." I inclined my head even though it was weird to use his first name. "I love chocolate. I love that you went to this much trouble, and if it's okay with you, I *will* want to take home a portion of everything."

He blinked at me. "Sure thing, Tyler."

"And I want to apologize for what I said at the school." There was more blinking, and my mom reached over the table past a tub of whipped cream for my hand and squeezed it tight. I didn't know if it was a warning, or encouragement, but either way, I wasn't stopping now. "You're not my dad, and you won't ever be my dad, because my dad was evil and hateful, and he made my mom cry every single day."

Mom gasped. "Tyler—"

"No, Mom. It's true. And, Jim, if you make my mom happy, then as far as I'm concerned, we're family, and I hope Felix isn't being a moody ass because he has an issue with you dating my mom?"

Felix glanced at me in shock. "Of course, I don't," he mumbled. "I love your mom being with Dad." He tilted his chin. "They're happy, and I want that for my dad."

Opposite me, Mom was all teary.

"So, please, I didn't mean to snap at you, Jim, okay?"

"Okay."

"Also, sometimes, I might want a dad's advice, and maybe you can be there when I do, if that's okay with Felix."

At least Felix nodded, which was something.

Jim's mouth opened, and his eyes were as bright as my mom's. "Always."

"And Felix?"

Felix jumped as if I'd thrown water at him, his eyes widening. "What?" he asked cautiously. "I said it was okay."

"Not about that. I mean, what is your freaking problem?"

"I don't have a problem," he defended, but after having so much of him getting in my face, I'd learned to read Felix.

"If this is the bullying thing, then we all do things to survive high school, and I trust that you won't hurt me now. Or let anyone else hurt me. But if we can't get past this thing where you won't even look at me, then I don't know what to do."

Jeez. Where was all this bravery coming from?

"I'm sorry," Felix muttered, then stood so fast his chair slid on the wooden floor and hit a side table. "I'm sorry!" he shouted, and then he left the room.

Now what? I glanced at Jim, who stared at my mom, then after an unspoken discussion, stood.

"No, it's okay," I said. "I'll go after him."

Jim immediately picked up a plate and slid pie onto it. "He likes the pumpkin one," he said, then added a chocolate slice. I pocketed two forks, then wasn't sure where to go. "Yard, at the back past the vegetables."

I headed through the kitchen, slipped out of the back door, and found Felix faster than I would have at his last house with its sprawl of manicured gardens. He was standing by a bench, his back to me, talking on his phone. Man, it was cold out here. I should have grabbed my coat.

"… I don't know. What if Jonah tells him some of the things I said? What if all I've done has messed up my dad being happy. How do I tell Tyler …" He listened to whatever the other person was saying. "But babe…"

Ah, he's talking to Soren.

"Tell me what?" I asked loudly, and he flailed with the phone, only catching it at the last moment before it crashed to the gravel, then spun to face me. "Here, I have pie."

He ended the call to Soren with a quick goodbye, and took the plate I waggled at him, and we both sat down. I passed him a fork and encouraged him to take a bite, which he did. I sure hoped he eat fast, or we'd be frozen to this bench.

"Mom makes the best pie," I informed him, and he nodded. "So, what do you want to tell me."

"Nothing, I mean… if I… I don't want this to ruin what my dad has…"

"Spit it out, Felix."

"Jonah knows *everything* I said about you. I mean, all the stuff that Miles agreed with, that he encouraged in me." His eyes widened. "Not that I'm blaming Miles, it was all me, but I… shit…"

"Eat more pie," I demanded, and he did. Meanwhile, I took my first bite of whatever the chocolate one was—basically heaven wrapped in cream. We sat quietly for a while, and Felix went from stiff to calm and back to stiff again.

"I dress like a girl," I announced.

He spluttered. "No, you don't!" His defense was immediate. "You dress like you. Perfect and just… you. I love that you can know yourself and have that strength of conviction, and the way you do your eyes, and how you can go out on the ice and put up with people's garbage words and… shit…" He subsided, as if he'd abruptly understood why I'd said that—to goad him into a reaction.

"See, I bet you used to say that girl thing about me behind my back, same as you did to my face. I know Miles said it directly at me at the Halloween dance, and I told him my mom was a girl and that she was stronger than all of us. Anyway, what's wrong with a boy wanting to feel pretty, and show their feminine side, and wear nail polish, huh?"

"Nothing," Felix said, then sighed. "Shit, Tyler. I said a lot of things, and if you're friends with Jonah and he hates me, then he'll tell you all the things I thought and said, and then you'll hate me, and yet again, I've fucked up things for my dad, and—"

"This isn't about you, so stop making it that way," I said sharply.

He opened his mouth, then shut it again, giving me a quick nod.

"As to Jonah? He doesn't hate you. He understands, okay? He's my friend, and he's a kind person, someone who did what they needed to do at the time to survive being thrown in at the deep end. Sound familiar? I'm not condoning what he did, or what you did. I don't understand it, but I know he regrets everything, and I know you do too, and it's that part I'm holding on to."

"Jonah wasn't like Miles, or me, he was…" Felix searched for the right word. "Trapped. And I wouldn't let him go."

Silence.

I needed to break the silent stalemate somehow.

"You want to know something?" I asked.

"What?"

"I have a guaranteed way to beat everyone at Monopoly." He seemed confused at the change in subject, and I smiled at him. "I bet you I can bankrupt you, and our parents, in the space of an hour."

His eyes narrowed. "There's no way to guarantee a win—"

"Oh, there is." I studied my nails. "Wanna try me?"

"You're on," he said, his competitive nature coming to the fore.

We headed back to the house, but he stopped me just by the door. "Look, before we go in..." He paused and drew a deep breath. "The guilt is real, and then I feel guilty because I'm pushing that guilt onto you and making you deal with the guilt that you shouldn't even have to deal with because it's my guilt and it shouldn't affect you." Everything tumbled out in a mess, but he seemed relieved it was out.

I fake-punched his arm. "Well, I won't feel guilty when I take all your houses and your money and leave you weeping at the side of the board. So, suck it up, Mr. McGuilty."

When we got inside, Mom and Jim jumped apart from where they'd been clearing the kitchen, aka kissing, and stared at us expectantly.

I pointed at Jim and Mom. "You two, me, Felix, Monopoly."

Mom chuckled. "After we do the dishes," she warned.

I shrugged. "See, Felix? Mom knows I'm gonna win and will do anything to delay the inevitable."

AN HOUR AND TWENTY MINUTES LATER, I SENT A photo to Jonah. Huddled around the Monopoly board, Jim was fake-crying, Mom fake-angry, Felix with his mouth open in shock, and me holding all of the money along with a handful of all of the houses and hotels.

Tyler: *Too much turkey, too much chocolate, but I own them all. #ThanksgivingBillionaire #Chocolate #SuckItFam*

Then, I waited a moment as we all collected ourselves, and Mom and Jim vanished to make drinks and bring in yet more pie. This time, I took a selfie of me and Felix, who by now was studying the Monopoly rules as if there was a cheat code and sent the image to the Coyotes Group Chat.

Tyler: *Loser with a capital L. #Loser #BiggestLoser #IWin*

A flurry of messages came back, but it was the

response to the family photo I'd sent to Jonah that I looked for first.

Jonah: *I love that photo. All good?*

Tyler: *So much good. So good that it's the goodest.*

Jonah: …

I watched the dots dance, wondering what Jonah had to say that seemed to take forever. It would probably end up being a simple emoji, and then the messages would stop until I got home. Only it wasn't an emoji at all.

Jonah: *I miss you, Tyler.*

Jonah: *And I wish I was there with you, or that you were here with me.*

Wow, that was a loaded message. I stared at it, fending off Felix with one hand as he began to explain how Monopoly actually worked—hey, I never said I played by the rules. I typed out the message I'd been wanting to send since the moment we started messaging.

Tyler: *I like you.*

Jonah: *I like you, too.*

Tyler: *I mean I like you a lot.*

Dancing dots… more dancing dots… and I finally got away from Felix's revenge tackles by hiding in the bathroom. Dude should know I'm faster than him.

Jonah: *I like you a lot, too. A real lot of like.*

"I know you're in there, cheater!" Felix banged on the door. "I'm taking away all your pie!"

Oh. That was war. I sent a quick message back, a simple *X*, and pocketed the phone, opened the door, and got hit in the face with a spoonful of Cool Whip.

"You're dead!" I announced.

And so, the food war began.

Chapter Eleven

Jonah

THE LAST GAME THE COYOTES PLAYED BEFORE winter break was against Hershey, at home, and the joint was rocking.

Every seat at the rink was filled, mostly with Coyote backers. There were some boosters from Hershey as well, but the majority of people in the stands were here for the home team. The vibe was upbeat. The team was fired up. Coach had given an amazing pep talk a few minutes ago, calling out his inner Herb Brooks in a big way. Every man in that locker room, including me and I wasn't even wearing skates, was ready to rumble. Rumble as in play good hockey, not fight. Fighting was not allowed in high school hockey. Players and parents had to sign agreements that forbade violence of any type—on and off the ice—so the punishments for doing so were strict. Like, expulsion or being barred from playing sports to criminal charges. Kind of like what Miles was now possibly facing for hitting me on school grounds.

Also, Coach frowned on using your fists to win a game, though throwing down the gloves was part of the game at higher levels. He liked to say that skill, speed, and smarts won hockey games, not haymakers.

I'd been snapping images like mad throughout the pregame talk, forcing myself to ensure I took pictures of everyone, not just Tyler. It was hard. He was naturally photogenic. Pretty even, and that prettiness played out well in pictures. His cheekbones were supermodel sharp, his eyes bright green with thick lashes, and his lips…

Yeah, I had to stop thinking about his lips. I so wanted to kiss them but wasn't sure how to go about making a move. I'd kissed a few girls before. Even gone a little further, but I'd never been this attracted to a dude that I could actually, maybe, kiss. Like, sure, I had imagined what it would be like to plant a lip-lock on Jung Kook from BTS, but that was not likely to ever happen. Kissing Tyler though…

Maybe. Someday. If I could ever find the nerve.

"Okay, team, this is a big game," Shaun was saying as I shook off the smooching fantasies. He thunked around the locker room, ready for battle, his helmet already on. It was hard to see his face well with the full face cage, but you could see his eyes burning with intensity though the grid. "Hershey is tied with us for first. If we can beat them tonight, we go into the break with the lead. Talk about a freaking awesome early gift from Santa!"

The guys all hooted, pumped the air, and started shouting "Ho-Ho-Ho, Hershey has got to go!' as they all thundered out to the ice. I danced around the team, snapping shot after shot, until they hit the ice, then I had to move to the side. I'd spend most of the game behind the bench with the coaching staff. Mom and Dad had had to sign a waiver for me to be there. In case I took a puck to the face or something. Since I was still sporting some bruising from the Miles incident, I looked like that had already happened.

The school choir sang the national anthem. Coach reminded the guys to play fair, play smart, and play hard. The first line was on the ice for the initial puck drop of the game. Hershey was a good team, fast and skilled, but so were we. And we had Tyler, who was so quick that the bigger defensemen had their hands full trying to contain him.

Shaun was the first line center, a huge guy with all the skills to take him to the pros. He was five-eleven already, at only sixteen. College reps had spoken to him and his parents. I mean, it was crazy he was being courted before he even graduated high school, but that was how good he was. And he had that certain spark team captains needed. He lived and breathed the game. He was cute, smart, outgoing, and definitely aiming for the NHL.

The bench erupted with angry shouts when a Hershey player knocked Felix off his skates. Clean hit, totally, but you could tell that was hit number one of what would be a shit ton of checking. And yep, as the first period went on, the team began to bring out their best checks. Nothing dirty. Skates stayed on the ice. No shoulders or elbows flew. But man, the guys were hitting back with a vengeance. I got one shot of Shaun taking out a big Hershey winger with a hip check that bowled the guy over the boards into the laps of his teammates.

There was no score after two periods, which probably made Coach happy. He liked to see tight defense being played. When the third period started, I moved down to stand beside Coach and our volunteer coach, Shaun's dad, camera at the ready. Something had to break soon goal-wise. Or so I thought. Fifteen minutes later, the score was tied at zero, and we were headed into an eight minute overtime followed by a shoot-out if no one scored. The players got a three-minute break, changed ends of the ice, and we were back at it.

I wedged myself into a corner of the bench area, trained my camera on Tyler, and followed our speedster down the ice as soon as Shaun passed him the puck. He moved around a bigger player, flew up center ice, and outfoxed three Hershey players with an outstanding deke. The goalie was in position, but his glove hand was a fraction of a second too slow to catch the short shot Tyler got off after losing that trio of players.

The Coyote bench erupted as the red lamp was lit. I wanted to leap and shout, but I kept the lens on Tyler as he threw his hands into the air to celebrate. His expression was pure joy. It made me feel so good to see him so happy. If anyone deserved to be happy, it was Tyler. He was then buried under the bodies of his teammates as they piled on him. I snapped several dozen images of the celly, then lowered my camera to join in the shouts of joy filling the arena. I was so proud of Tyler, and all the Coyotes. They were more to me than just a project to get extra credit. They had become friends, mostly, and that was something I'd never had before. It felt good. Real good. I hoped we could maintain the tenuous friendship after my time as the team's unofficial photographer was done. Time would tell. Right now, it was celly and ramen noodle time, and yeah, being part of that felt super good too.

"Okay, so tell me, and be honest, did you learn those moves from watching hockey tapes?" I asked Tyler as we—we as in the team—settled into our seats at Hot Pot Noodle Shop.

"Yeah, kind of. I spend a lot of time watching films of Tennant Rowe, of course," Tyler said as he sat under a neon image of an anime hero using chopsticks as weapons and gave Soren a nod. Soren gave him a quick bow, then sat down beside Felix, who was forced to sit beside me. I scooted over a little, to give him as much room as possible. "Oh, and Pavel Datsyuk. That guy was amazing. They called him 'Magic Man,' and I wish I had one millionth of the skill he had with stick handling."

I sat back and smiled at Tyler. I knew the names

of the big league players, but not much more. Hockey wasn't a big sport in my house, but it was quickly growing into one of my top three faves. Coach was up at the register, telling the servers that everything for our long, loud table was on him. Which was really on the school, I assumed. It took two servers to take and then deliver our orders. The guys were vocal, still pumped from the win, and talk centered on everything, moving from one topic to another as appetizers, such as seaweed salad, steamed dumplings, and veggie sushi rolls, were eaten.

Main dishes arrived, most of them huge bowls of ramen served with a wooden spoon and chopsticks. There were platters of avocado bibimbap, kimchi, and tofu BBQ.

"Where's Shaun?" Soren asked. "His pickled radishes are here."

Felix glanced at him. "Last I saw, he was in a heated debate with his dad."

"Uh oh," was all Soren said, and the entire table took a moment to consider the words. I didn't know what was going on with that, but the somber mood shifted just as fast.

I felt at home with the guys and was trying to listen in on all the chatter, ignoring my soup to finally leave my seat to take shots of the party. The noodle shop was packed, and the high spirits of the team seemed to be contagious because everyone was loud and laughing. It was a great time, and sadly, it was over too soon. Most of the players began to file out as their rides arrived. It was getting late, and we did have school tomorrow. Granted, it was like a waster day as most of the teachers weren't doing anything since break started right after, but it was still an early rise. I returned to our table to take a sip of my iced tea.

Tyler and Soren were over at another table, chatting with some of the booster club kids, which left me and Felix alone. I poked at my cold chicken ramen soup with my chopsticks while he tapped on the empty plate that had held his vegan mochi donut. Everyone else had left, and Soren had offered to give us all a lift with his grandpa riding shotgun. We had an hour or so to kill. I thought of maybe beginning the long process of sorting through my pictures just to pass the time. Anything would be better than sitting here with Felix as we both wallowed in the bog of everlasting guilt.

"Okay, so I guess this is maybe on purpose," Felix said as a song from Lizzo began to play. The eatery was still hopping, but the older eaters had left. I glanced up from my chilly soup, lowering my chopsticks, to stare at him quizzically. "Them leaving us sitting here. I guess that's on purpose, so we can talk shit out."

"Oh." I glanced over to the booster table. Tyler caught my gaze, then gave me a subtle jerk of his head as if to say, "Talk to him" or something kind and sweet along those lines. "Yeah, probably."

"I guess they think if we sit here over cold soup and donut crumbs we can magically make things better," he huffed, his unease creeping into my once good feelings. "I'm not... Okay, so this is the thing." He finally looked at me. "We're a couple of assholes."

That stung, but yeah, he was right. "Ex-assholes," I felt needed to be said. One corner of his tense mouth lifted. "I mean, I'm trying to make shit right with Tyler, and my life. I know you are too."

"You know that?" He seemed genuinely surprised.

"Yeah, well, you're like a mother hippo or something."

"A hippo?"

"Yeah, hippos are the most dangerous land animals on the planet. They kill more people than lions, tigers, or sharks annually, so imagine that a mother hippo is pissed about you trying to pet her baby hippo."

He sat back to study me. "Where do you pull all of these rando animal facts from all the time?"

"I read *National Geographic*."

"Oh, I thought you just looked at the pictures."

"Well, I do that too. The point is that you've been hyper-protective of Tyler, which shows me that you're trying to clean up your shit. I am too, and I'm not going to allow anyone to hurt him again."

His bright eyes narrowed. "You sound like a boyfriend." His gaze flickered to the rubber bi colors bracelet on my wrist. I let him look. I wasn't hiding that part of me anymore. Brave talk from a guy who had yet to tell his parents he liked a guy. "Anything you want to tell me?"

"No, not really. It's private, but just know that I see you, Felix. I'll back off and let you get things worked out with Tyler. Miles, though, he's still an issue."

"He's probably going to get suspended, if not expelled. This isn't his first offense." I motioned to my face. "Hopefully, he'll be gone from our lives for good. I really want to get my shit straightened out; you know?"

"Yeah, I know." He held up his fist. I rapped it

lightly. Soren and Tyler miraculously appeared then, both beaming, as we lowered our hands to the table.

"Look at you two playing nice," Soren teased, bending down to kiss Felix on the cheek, then pulling him to the booster table to talk booster stuff.

Tyler sat down beside me, his eyes round, the neon light from a giant bowl of ramen making his pink hair glow red. It looked good. I was thinking any color of hair would be amazing on the guy.

"You two okay?" he asked, picking up my chopsticks, then fishing out some chicken to feed to me. I sat there stunned at the display of what I would say was something more than platonic.

"Uhm, we're okay. Not best friends or anything, but it's getting sorted." I opened my mouth, uncertain of how this was playing out, but kind of loving it. He fed me the chicken, nodded merrily, then fished out some noodles.

"Good, you two need to sort your shit. Here, eat. I've never seen anyone who forgets to take in calories like you do. Is that an artist thing? Forgetting to chow down when you're busy making art?"

"Maybe," I confessed, leaning over the table as he dribbled wet noodles to my mouth. I sucked them off the chopsticks. One long one flew up to smack me in the nose.

"Oh sorry!" He laughed, gathered more noodles, then lifted them high to try to catch the end of one mile-long strand. I watched in amusement as he captured the wayward noodle, then rolled his eyes from the cold noodles to me. "Get the other end," he whispered around his noodle, his lips puckered slightly as he began to gently pull it into his mouth. Heart hammering, I pushed up to kneel on my seat, one knee on the chair, one foot on the ground, and captured the whole clump at once. The broth ran down my chin as we both sucked on that one long noodle, the raucous patrons, servers, and glowing neon fading away as his pink lips touched mine. I'd seen this scene before, but it had been two dogs and spaghetti. Two guys and ramen worked, too. It worked *really* super well. His lips were soft, and warm, and tasted of spicy chicken ramen. Which was now, and would forever be, my favorite soup in the world, bar none.

We drew back, cheeks flaming red, chins wet with broth, and smiled stupidly at each other.

"That was really nice," Tyler said, his emerald eyes glowing.

I was about to reply with something similar, as well as a request to do it again, when the tiny bells over the front door rang, and a voice I had hoped to never hear again filled the happy noodle shop.

"Guess this is the last time I eat here. I'd hate to get faggot germs all over me," Miles called so loudly his hateful words were probably heard back in the boisterous kitchen.

Chapter Twelve

Tyler

I GRABBED A NAPKIN AND WIPED MY FACE, ALL MY happy thoughts vanishing in an instant as soon as Miles's toxic hate filled the restaurant. Opposite me, Jonah stiffened, his smile dropping just as fast.

"It's okay," he quickly reassured me. "Ignore him."

Easier said than done when Miles and his small group took the table next to us, and all four of them lounged back in their chairs, sprawling as if they owned the place. Miles was in his usual post-school outfit of jeans and a white T-shirt, his hair freshly buzzed, his sneer so familiar it made my stomach knot. Where was the bravery I'd used to face up to him at school, because right now, I felt vulnerable and exposed and pissed that he'd interrupted my happy time with Jonah.

Plus, the guilt was real, from seeing Jonah get hit, knowing it was me who'd caused it, understanding that if I'd only walked away that time, then Jonah wouldn't still be sporting bruises. Guilt was the worst thing ever, and I glanced at Jonah to see that he was tense and ready to fight.

Please. No more fighting.

Miles clapped his hands together as if he was calling for attention. "Hey, Jonah, my man, does he know you called him a fag behind his back?"

"I'm not your man," Jonah snapped back, but he seemed to shrink in on himself.

Still Miles went on with his vitriol. "Hey, you remember the time we trapped the pink-haired twink in the bathroom and the little pussy cried?"

Jonah sent me a stricken glance, his eyes bright with emotion, his skin pale. I remembered the day of being locked in the bathroom well, but I don't recall crying or Jonah being part of it. Was I recalling that scenario through rose-tinted glasses and forgetting Jonah was there?

Stop it. He's changed.

"Whatever," I said loudly, and by that time Soren

and Felix had left the booster club table and were standing next to *me*. Didn't they realize it wasn't me who needed help?

"Ignore him," I told Jonah and pushed the noodle bowl out of the way. "Let's go." We both stood, the four of us heading to the door, but then, Jonah stepped back, and it startled me. I realized it wasn't him moving away from us, but Miles dragging at his shirt. I spun to face Miles, but he was already up in Jonah's face, muttering something awful by Jonah's expression, and now it was my turn to get between Miles and Jonah. Only Soren and Felix got there first and backed me and Jonah out of the door into the fresh air. Miles followed us, but I'd reached my limit on the hate he was dishing out to the world. I shoved past Soren, stepped right into Miles's space, toe to toe, waiting for him to hit me this time.

Ready for it.

"Fuck off!" I shouted in the asshole's face.

"Oh, look at the little boy getting all up in my face," he taunted, before it turned evil. "It was your *boyfriend* who locked the door," Miles said with what looked like glee. "Locked you in there, and then laughed at you, said you were pathetic, called you a waste of air." He snarled the last part. I was aware that Felix and Soren were on my right. I couldn't sense Jonah, but there was no way I was letting Jonah take another punch for me.

"He didn't!"

"Ask him," Miles sneered and snorted a laugh. "And you think he wants to kiss you? He's not a fucking fag!"

Tension snapped, and I moved my body weight, winding up into throwing a punch, but someone caught my arm, and flanked by Soren and Felix, it was Jonah who stepped between me and Miles.

"You're being recorded," Jonah said clearly, then indicated the entire booster club with their phones out. "I'd like you to leave us alone now." Jonah wasn't losing his cool. He wasn't defending with fists and fury. He was icy calm, and I peered around him.

Miles laughed again—there was nothing but darkness in that sound.

"Pretend all you like, loser," Miles poked at Jonah's chest. "But you're the same as me." Then, he turned to go back into Hot Pot.

In the chaos that came next, with the entire booster club surrounding us, talking over each other, swapping recordings and numbers, I lost sight of Jonah, and when everyone walked away, leaving me with Soren and Felix, I couldn't see Jonah at all. He'd gone.

"Jonah said we should make sure you get home okay," Felix explained, but wouldn't meet my gaze.

"Where did he go?"

Soren shrugged. "He… I don't know."

Fear gripped me. "Is he inside?" I yanked Soren out of the way. "Did he go back in?"

Soren took my arm and tugged me back from the door to where a car waited, his grandpa in the driving seat. "Let's get you home."

"No." I pulled my arm free. "I need to find Jonah."

Felix crowded me with Soren, then sighed. "He said he was going home; he said we should make sure you got back to your place okay. That's it."

"Coming boys?" Soren's grandpa called, and I was torn. What did I do now? Jonah had gone home, left the scene once he knew I was okay, and the last expression I'd seen on his face was misery. Abject desolation and guilt consuming him. What had Miles whispered to him?

"No. I need to… he probably thinks I believe what Miles said." I faced Felix head-on. "It's not true, because that's not him; that's not the Jonah that I…"

That I what?

My cell vibrated, and I juggled it to read the

screen. The message was from Jonah, short and to the point.

"Gone home," I read out. "Talk tomorrow." Another message came through as I read the first. "If you want to." He'd added that last bit, and I could feel his regret in those few words. Of course, I wanted to talk to him—I refused to believe this was anything other than Miles stirring things up.

I wasn't wrong about Jonah. I wasn't stupid. I knew Jonah had found his way now, and I trusted him.

When Soren's grandpa dropped me at my door, I thanked him, said my goodbyes, and headed in to find Mom curled on the sofa with a book, music playing softly in the background. She'd made a haven for us, a protective space where we could restart our family, but even that didn't calm my worries as I sank onto the sofa next to her, my phone in my hand.

"Good game tonight," she said and nudged my arm. "That goal was amazing. I'm so proud."

I leaned on her, then she tucked me into her side. How many times had we sat here, hugging each other, and making everything right because of another bully? Because of Dad? So many in the times he'd been here, and so many since he'd left. We'd found a new peace, of sorts, both craving something in our lives that was happier. She'd found it with Felix's dad, I think, and I was on my way to finding a new me in the mess of school and love of hockey.

"Are you okay, sweetheart?" she asked after a while.

I gripped my phone hard. "Do you think you'll ever forgive Dad for what he did to you?"

She stiffened momentarily. "Why do you ask that? Has something happened? Is it your dad? Is he contacting you?"

"No to Dad." I paused. "But…" I sighed and burrowed deeper, and she held me tight. "I like Jonah. A lot. I thought he was… I thought I could… I've kissed him."

She knew who Jonah was—that wasn't the issue, it was that she would never be able to forgive any of them for making me cry. She was struggling with Felix, but making the effort, and always asking me if it was okay.

"You kissed him?" She didn't sound shocked, or angry.

"And he's not who you think he is."

"Okay."

"He's trying so hard to be a different person, and I think I'm falling for the genuine parts of him."

"There sounds like you have a but?"

Was there a but? Not about my growing attraction to Jonah, but about what had happened tonight. "Miles was at Hot Pot, and he said some things about what Jonah had done, and he whispered stuff I couldn't hear, and then, Jonah left."

Mom stayed quiet for a while. "He left you with Miles?" If anything, she was even tenser now, on the brink of anger, or maybe knee-deep in it already.

"No, he stood up for me again, but the broken parts of him were right there, all the guilt and anxiety, and parts we'd been so close to understanding. He says he'll see me in the morning, but then, he added a bit about *if I wanted*. Of course, I want to."

"Be careful," she warned gently. "Look out for yourself in all of this, trust your instincts, don't…" She stopped and hugged me tightly. I knew what she was going to say. *Don't be the victim; don't let yourself be manipulated, or worse, hurt so bad that everything was painful.*

"I won't," I promised. I eased away from her, and she was crying. Not huge gasping emotions falling out of her, but silent tears that were somehow worse. Dad wasn't part of our lives anymore, but his hold on her would never ease entirely. I'd seen her crying before, and every time, I'd just held her and loved her completely. That didn't mean I wanted to see her cry now.

"You like Felix, right?"

She curled back in the corner and nodded. "I like his dad a lot, and I'm attempting not to hold onto the bad feelings about Felix for what he did to you, for seeing past the pain that child carried, and seeing him for the person he could be. He's kind to you now, and you've forgiven him, so I'm trying. But Jonah… I don't know him well enough." She tapped her knee absently. "Invite him for dinner. Saturday."

"I'm not sure where we'll be at by then," I said, sadly, knowing he was probably reliving all the things he'd been part of and thinking I hated him, and that I believed what Miles said. "But I'm determined to get him to visit."

Mom kissed the top of my head. "I'll make pot roast. Just for the three of us."

"Thanks, Mom."

"And you want some advice?" she asked.

"Always."

"If he believes you think bad of him, and you truly don't? Change his mind."

With my mom's advice ringing in my ears, I sent a message to Jonah, hoping he had his phone with him and hadn't thrown it out of his window.

Although, why he'd do that I don't know, but never let it be said I lacked imagination.

Tyler: *Dinner Saturday. My mom's making pot roast.*

Nothing.

Tyler: *Did you get the message?*

Tyler: *Answer me if you can.*

Tyler: *I don't believe a thing Miles said.*

Still nothing. Not bouncing dots or ticks to indicate he'd read what I wrote. I sighed but was utterly determined he didn't go to bed thinking we were done.

Tyler: *Unlock your phone Jonah!*

Tyler: *Jonah!*

Tyler: *Jonah!*

Tyler: *Jonah!*

Tyler: *Unlock your phone!*

I was so busy typing the next annoying message that I missed the bouncing dots, and the waterfall of green ticks showing he'd read each one. I backspaced my obnoxiously annoying pokes at him and changed the message.

Tyler: *Are you there?*

Stupid question given I knew he was there now, but still, it was something to type.

Jonah: *We can talk tomorrow.*

Well, that was a shit message. I wasn't ready to wait until tomorrow. So, I video called him, and even though it took a few rings, he finally answered, and I could see the caution in him as I propped my phone on my knee. Not the most flattering view for him to see, but I needed the use of my hands if I was going to persuade him to listen to me.

"Hi," I said. Great start, not.

"Is everything okay?" Jonah asked immediately. "I told Soren and Felix to look out for you—"

"I would have been far happier if you'd stayed," I interrupted and pointed at him. "Whatever Miles said was just a steaming pile of nothing."

Jonah blanched. "I know. I promise you I wouldn't have used those words or locked you anywhere, but..." He stopped and rubbed his face with one hand, the phone wobbling. "I was still part of it."

"I see." I waited a beat. "So, every time Miles pops up, you're going to think I don't want to be near you anymore?"

"Wait, no. This isn't about me; this is about you. How can you even want to kiss someone like me, who didn't intervene when—"

"Because you're cute. And smile at me. And you smell nice. And you protected me. And you don't really have an evil bone in your body. And I like you a lot. And I want to kiss you again."

He blinked at me. "Oh."

"And if we have things to work through, well maybe, we won't have to worry about Miles much longer, and I wouldn't even know where to start with telling you about my dad, and then, the noodle thing was so sweet." I know that all came out in a jumble of things, but it made Jonah's lips curve a little.

"I still want to talk," he said after a short pause.

"Maybe Saturday, okay? Come over at four or so, we have a pool. It's not a big one, or fancy, but it's a pool. You like swimming, right?"

"Sure I—"

"Bring stuff, and when we've done the pool thing, and the food thing, then, we find a dark corner and kiss some more, and do the whole talking thing?"

"Okay."

"I think I like you more than just the like that I liked you before."

He smiled then, cautiously. "How can you…" He stopped. "I think the same."

I blew him a kiss then, and he blushed, and then, it was time to go, and I hoped I'd done enough for him to not sit there stewing over what happened tonight.

Chapter Thirteen

Jonah

SOMETIMES, I THINK PARENTS HAVE MIND-READING capabilities.

I'd just ended the call with Tyler when my mother knocked three times on the door. That was her serious knock sequence. One knock was to turn down my music. Two was to turn out my light and go to bed. Three meant she was sensing something in that mom-worry space in her head. I rolled to my side, then called for her to enter.

She slipped inside, the dim glow of a nightlight in the hall illuminating her from behind. She was in her pajamas, a thick flannel top and pants with green pine trees and candy canes. Mom was big on Christmas.

How she and Dad managed to give all four of us what we asked for every year was a real holiday miracle. I bet they had all their credit cards maxed out, which was why I only mentioned a new hoodie and maybe having a boyfriend named Tyler on my wish list. The girls had lists for Santa that ran from here to the capitol building. The boyfriend wish was private, between me and Saint Nick.

"Hey, you need to talk?" She moved into the room, closed the door, and walked over to sit beside me on the bed. She started rubbing my arm. "I saw your face when you came in. You didn't say hello to Dad and me, so I assumed something bad happened after that big win."

I blew out a breath. The door cracked open. We both glanced away from each other expecting to see my baby sister, but it was my father peeking around the door.

"You two having a heart-to-heart?" he asked, easing the door open, but not coming in. "I was going to offer to make some hot chocolate and dish up some of those sugar cookies."

"Terrence, those cookies are for the rec center senior party tomorrow night," she said.

"Oops," Dad whispered, then hurried to swipe at the sprinkles on his lips. "You didn't see that."

I chuckled, then sat up, pulling my knees to my chest, and hugging them tight, as they mock-wrangled with each other about cookies. My folks were really cool for the most part. Sure, they were kind of cheesy at times, like with my mom's Bowie adoration and my dad's off-key singing of old songs, but they were good people. And I was not. The bit of good humor that they'd brought out dimmed as I recalled what Miles had said tonight.

"I think I'm a really terrible human being," I coughed out. Dad and Mom both stopped the cookie talk. Mom pulled me in for a hug. Dad sat beside me. And I started crying, my head resting on my knees, all the crap that was my life came bubbling out of me like a backed-up sewer.

"Honey, you are not a bad person; you're a good young man who just got a little sidetracked," Mom cooed, moving her hands in wide tender circles on my heaving back. "We all fumble around in life, baby. Just because you make mistakes doesn't mean you can't learn from them. That's what it's all about. Learning from our mistakes. Isn't that right, Terrence?"

"Yeah, totally. Heck, Jonah, if you knew half the stupid shit I did at your age, well, let's just say there's a reason my mother has gray hair."

"Your father was a bit of a hellion when he was younger," Mom confided. "Tell him about the time that you and your cousin Leon stole your grandfather's produce delivery truck, then drove around town chucking veggies at your neighbor's house."

That brought my head up. Dad was skewering Mom with a look. "I don't figure I have to tell him since you just did. In my defense, it was mischief night, and Leon was driving."

I swiped at my face. "Did you get into trouble?"

"Oh, hell yes," Dad laughed, then quickly cleared the amusement from his face. "Neither of us had licenses. Why not ask your mother about the time she and Aunt Nelly were caught smoking Virginia Slims behind the 7-11 when they were thirteen."

My sight flew to my mother. "Mom?" I gasped because she was super against smoking.

She threw a flat expression at my father. "We're not talking about smoking, Terrence."

"We weren't talking about throwing rotten rutabagas at Old Man Wilkes' door either, but there it is."

"The point that we're trying to make is that we all stray off the path on occasion, but that doesn't mean we're bad people. It just means were human, honey," Mom said.

Dad handed me his hankie. I blew and wiped and blew some more, then tucked it under my butt for later because I was overwhelmed.

"I kissed a boy tonight," I whispered, staring at the knees of my jeans. Total and utter silence fell over my room. I didn't dare look up. I knew I'd see all kinds of disgust on my parents' faces, and after the shit with Miles I—

"Was it Tyler?" Mom asked. A small atomic detonation took place inside my skull. No kidding, they could probs see tiny cartoon mushroom clouds leaking out of my ears. My sight flew from my knees to my mother. She smiled in that kind mom way that made me cry a little bit more. "Oh, honey, there's no need to cry. Your dad and I suspected there was something more to you and Tyler than just friends. The way you look at him is pretty telling." She patted my back as I struggled to drink all that in.

"So, like… you knew?"

"We suspected. Also, you started wearing a bi bracelet, which was a big tell," Dad said, reaching over to drape his arm around my shoulders. "Did you get consent?"

"It was kind of a mutual thing," I confessed, my

cheeks burning hot. "We had noodles and… total Disney thing. And it was amazing, and I wanted another kiss, then Miles showed up and starting tossing around the f-word."

"I swear that kid needs a firm size thirteen right up his—"

"Terrence, violence solves nothing," Mom was quick to say, but I could see the ire in her blue eyes. "I hope you boys ignored him. He's in quite a bit of trouble as it is without harassing you in public places. Maybe we should file a restraining order or something."

"No! God, no, please, nothing like that. We handled it, me and the guys, and the booster club. There are videos of him getting in our faces all over social media. I just…" I blew out a breath, then scrubbed at my face with the tips of my fingers. Dad gave my neck a soft squeeze while Mom continued holding me to her side. Were there any hugs better than Mom hugs? "I just… he said things that were really shitty. Sorry, crappy. Really crappy, but all true. About how I just let kids get bullied, how I called people names and slurs. Not racial slurs, but queer slurs. Then, he leaned in real close and said that I was a dirty N word F word."

Dad shot to his feet. "That's it. Size thirteen in the keister time!"

"Terrence, sit *down*. Please." Dad sat, but he was muttering hotly under his breath about buying steel-toed boots just for the upcoming ass-kicking. Mom turned her attention back to me. "Jonah, we've taught you that words are just words. They mean nothing. I know they hurt, and I know that they're used as weapons, but you have a shield against bad words. That shield is knowing your self-worth, something that racist homophobes have no clue about because they hate themselves more than they hate others. You are a good, strong, smart young man. That Miles wishes he had what you have."

"I don't think he wants to kiss guys," I replied, then sagged into her arms even more.

"That's his loss then. I think kissing guys is fun. So does your father."

Dad choked on his spit. My eyes flew from Mom's shoulder to my dad.

"Okay, so I think that might have been taken out of context. What I said was that, if I were into men, I would so plant a lip-lock on Idris Elba," Dad explained while Mom gave him a soft little glance that was all "Uh-huh, you'd so do Idris," and really who wouldn't? "But I'm only into your mom, so there is no kissing on Luther-slash-Heimdall."

Mom kissed my head. "You just go on being the best Jonah you can be. And ignore that dickhead Miles and his brat pack." Dad snorted. "The girls are all in bed, so they didn't hear it, and it's the truth."

"Massive walking peen," I commented from my mom's strong shoulder. "Tyler is cool with me, which I don't get. Why is he so okay with all the shit that I did to him?"

"I'd say because he was raised right and taught that empathy and forgiveness are gracious gifts to bestow on those who are trying to better themselves," Mom whispered as she hugged me tight. "I'm glad you have him on your side now, and the other boys on the team, too."

"Even Felix?" I asked, and Dad made the same sound he makes when he sees the neighbor's dog using our yard for a toilet.

"Felix is a work in progress for us, but yes, even Felix. See, even us old people can strive to better ourselves." She lifted my face from her shoulder and kissed my cheek. "Now, why don't I bring you some warm milk and cookies, then you can get some rest. Winter break starts tomorrow, and I'm sure you have big plans with your new friends."

"Tyler asked me to go to his place and swim on Saturday," I confessed as they slowly stood. Mom shot a look at Dad. "They have a heated pool."

"That's lovely," Mom replied with sincerity. I knew, probably, deep down, she was maybe feeling a twinge of jealousy, but she wasn't letting it darken her soul.

"Why does he get the okay on the cookies, but I caught the dickens?" Dad asked, giving me a wink as he followed Mom out the door.

"Because he's my baby boy," Mom tossed over her shoulder.

"Yeah, but if you give me a few more cookies we can go to our room and y'know…" Dad replied, easing up behind Mom to grab her butt. They both ran out of my room giggling like freshman girls who'd wandered into the swim team locker room by mistake.

There were some things that a young man should not see or hear. One thing a young man *should* see and hear is that his parents love and accept him no matter who he dates. Also, that he's still got a guy who is willing to date him—maybe—even after that young man has been a royal scrotum.

TYLER'S HOUSE WAS BIGGER THAN OURS, AND I KNEW he and his mom had moved back into the old family home—his dad off somewhere, and the judge ruling the property was his moms. I knew that because Soren had told me, in that warning-me-not-to-overreact kind of way.

Roomy and quiet. No little girls screaming all day long. I loved my sisters, but man did little girls scream. All the time, for like, no good reason. Mad? Scream. Sad? Scream. Happy? Scream. Hungry? Scream. So much screaming. Also, there were no hair barrettes, tiny cheese fish crackers, or Barbie shoes anywhere to be seen. Nothing but nice, new furniture, shiny floors, and one mom who was smiling way too hard.

"Thank you for having me over," I said as politely as I could to Mrs. Corrigan as Tyler stood at my side, worriedly working his lower lip. "My mom said to pass along that she and my dad are having a little party on Christmas Eve at our house, just a few couples, and that if you and Mr. Sinclair would like to come, you'd be more than welcome."

"Oh, that's so nice. Thank you. Yes, we'd love to come. Tell her I'll send her a friend request on Facebook, and we can settle the details."

"I will," I said right before Tyler took my wrist,

and hauled me to a small, enclosed room where we could get changed into our swimsuits in privacy.

"Sorry about Mom being so weird," Tyler called through the door of the bathroom/cabana-type space I was now stripping down in. Small little pictures of white sands and blue skies hung on the wall. There was a shower unit, some hooks by the door, and an off-white toilet. And a bidet. I stood there in my birthday suit staring at the bidet. Tyler's family had cash. If we had a bidet—which we wouldn't be able to afford since we still had the old toilet that made gurgling sounds in the upstairs bathroom—but if we ever did, my sisters would use it as a Barbie Dream Shower. No doubt in my mind.

Tyler was still talking. "She's still trying to get over the whole ugly past we have. At least we're back in the old house, better than an apartment, but it seems wrong for just me and mom."

I stepped into my trunks, sun-bleached from a summer spent at the local public pool. I opened the door, leaving my T-shirt on, and found Tyler playing with his hair. One pink strand was wrapped around his finger, his big green eyes moving up over my bare feet to my face. "I hope the pool is close."

"Yeah, just outside. It's nothing fancy, but…" he paused and dipped his gaze. "You look really nice."

"Oh, this old thing," I laughed as I plucked at my trunks. I was happy to see that the anxious look had left his face.

"I'm glad you're here." He rose to his bare toes to kiss me on the lips. A fast peck that made me giddy. He took my hand, and we raced outside. The temperature was a balmy fourteen degrees. My skin instantly broke into goosebumps as my naked feet hit the light dusting of snow on the patio. "Oh, shit, it's *freezing*!"

Tyler raced up the steps, and I ran after him, peeling off my T-shirt, then jumping into the water with a splash. Tyler was a quick swimmer, darting around the pool, and I had a time catching up to him. A wild and wooly game of Marco Polo broke out, the rules being that when you touched the other, you got to kiss them. I think Tyler had one eye cracked open since he found me too quickly to not be cheating. I wasn't complaining. When we wore ourselves out doing laps, Marco Polo, and a round of pool noodle combat that I won, we'd kissed about seventeen times.

Now, we were resting at the shallow end, steam rising around us, my sight on the solar panels on the roof as Tyler explained that was how they powered the house, as well as the heating units for the pool.

"My mom is big on trying to do our part," he explained as we sat on the lowest steps, the water tickling our chins. Well, *my* chin, Tyler was on the step behind me because he was shorter. His arms rested on my shoulders; his damp lips were beside my ear. It was really pretty perfect. "So, are we okay now?"

"Yeah, yeah, we're tight. I just wish I could go back in time and change things." I turned my head, and he pressed a kiss to the corner of my mouth. "I'd change so much. Do things differently. Not be such a massive dickwad."

"My mom says we all have regrets, but the challenge in life is to learn from them and better ourselves."

I smiled softly. "Your mom and my mom sound a lot alike."

"Yeah, moms speak a universal language I think."

That felt right. As did this moment here with his arms around me and the taste of cherry lip gloss and chlorine on my lips.

"You want something to eat?" Tyler asked.

"Nah, I'm good here." My stomach growled. Tyler giggled and my heart melted just like the snow bordering the pool.

Yeah, this was about as right as right could be.

Chapter Fourteen

Tyler

MOM'S CAUTION WAS LIKE A BEACON ACROSS THE table, and I knew she was trying at the start when we sat down, but now, she was quiet, and Jonah had also given up and was almost subdued. I was at a loss as to how to get the two of them talking and making a meaningful connection other than Jonah complimenting Mom on the food, and Mom telling him where she bought her groceries.

Not the kind of conversation I'd been hoping for.

What did they have in common? I wracked my brains for one thing. But I gave up when it turned out that Jonah did not, in fact, read romance mystery novels, or that my mom didn't get to the movies much at all.

I guess the only thing they had in common was me.

"Ouch," I said dramatically, and pressed a hand to my hip as if there was a lot of pain sitting in that spot.

Two sets of gazes flew my way, Jonah wide-eyed and Mom clearly already in mom-mode and considering what medical options she might have that fit my generic ouch.

"What's wrong?" she asked. "Is it your stomach?"

"No, my back," I said, and added a pathetic tone to my explanation, wincing and stretching.

"What happened to your back?" Mom asked. "Was it from hockey? Do we need to call someone?"

Jonah's assessment slipped out with no thought as to what my mom did and didn't need to hear. "I bet it was from when that ass from Hershey tipped him over the boards?"

"Oh my god, yes. I didn't like the way he did that," Mom added, directing her words at Jonah.

"Me neither. There was no need to keep pushing."

"Were you closer? Did you see Tyler get hurt?"

"I didn't know that he *was* hurt." Jonah sent me a look of accusation that I hadn't shared my injury with him. Given it was made up, I couldn't even defend myself.

"It didn't hurt until now," I said.

"Delayed shock," Mom said, in her most dramatic tone.

"I have the whole thing on closeup, hang on." Jonah put down his cutlery and fished out his phone, thumbing through to videos, then holding the cell out for my mom, who took it immediately.

"Oh my god, Tyler!" she exclaimed as she watched the incredibly clean, and not at all painful, hit from one of the Hershey defensemen, a big dude with an ever-present snarl. "It didn't look this bad from my angle."

Jonah leaned across and paused the video. "See what he did there? There was no need for that extra shove to tip Tyler into the home bench. That's probably where Tyler got injured."

"Tyler, why didn't you say you'd been in an accident like this? No wonder your back hurts. We should get you to urgent care for an X-ray."

"Did you hit your head?" Jonah asked.

"Why didn't you tell me!" Mom added.

Oh wow, this was all of a sudden getting out of hand. I'd only wanted them to connect with each other, not mother me. "It's not that bad—"

"And then see what that as—skater did? Keep watching." Jonah was really getting into this autopsy of what had been a very simple hit.

Mom's lips thinned as she watched it all again. "That's it. I'm talking to Coach Sennett about keeping you out for a while," Mom announced.

Oh hell no.

"I lied," I said in desperation.

They stared at me again, but this time, it was all confusion.

"Lied about what?" Mom frowned; Jonah raised an eyebrow.

"My back is fine. I'm fine; it's all good. But the only thing you have in common is me, and it was a conversation-starter because you're sitting here all awkward, and I didn't want it to be awkward. Mom, you need to talk to Jonah, and try to get to know him because he'll be around for a long time, and, Jonah, please say something about something... I mean anything would be good."

Jonah bit his lip, and he and Mom exchanged glances. Was he going to make a dramatic speech about how he was sorry about hanging around with Felix, and how things were changing, and he was changing and...

But no.

"I have more photos of Tyler. Do you want to see them?"

This was not where I had seen things going, but when he pointed out that all my mom needed to do was scroll in the folder she was looking at, then boy did she scroll. I helped myself to more chocolate dessert, and scraped my plate until it was completely clean, and in that time, Jonah had moved around to sit next to my mom, the two of them huddled over the phone.

"I can send you a copy of anything you want," Jonah said. "Also, I did some in black and white, do you want those?"

"I want them all," Mom announced, and glanced over at me. "Jonah is gifted at capturing images of you," she said, and I nodded. Something passed between us, an unspoken discussion about Jonah that ended with her offering me a cautious smile. Then, the smile turned devious. "Jonah, do you want to see some photos I have?" she asked, and I about died on the spot.

"Not the baby photos, Mom," I said quickly.

But she'd already left the table and headed for the study, Jonah in her wake. I left them to it, clearing the table, smiling whenever I heard laughter from what used to be my dad's domain, generally after Mom commented on something I was doing, or wearing, or eating, in all my toddler photos. When Dad had left just after my ninth birthday, the two of us had stripped that room of everything, right back to the sheetrock, and we'd painted the whole room in shades of pink and purple. There were still handprints from where we'd had a paint fight, never removed because each mark meant something. Now, there were beanbags in there, and buckets of photos and games, and it was ours. What used to be the evil center of the house had become a safe space.

I loaded the dishwasher, then ambled down the hall, catching my name, and stopping outside where they couldn't see me. I didn't want to interrupt any kind of bonding that might be happening.

"… I know," my mom finished, although other than my name, I hadn't caught much of what she said.

"It's all on me," I heard Jonah say. "If I'd been stronger, or more determined, hadn't been so stupidly scared for no reason… I let Tyler down, even though I wanted to be a friend, and I wish I could go back and for it all to be different."

"Oh, Jonah," Mom said and then, it went quiet for a while. "I wish you could go back as well. He's seen enough in his life, which makes it so hard for me to…" She stopped talking. "Just promise me you'll be good for him."

"Always," Jonah replied.

I tiptoed back to the kitchen, then called out to ask if anyone wanted a drink. The two of them came out of the study, and I acted as if I hadn't heard Jonah pouring his heart out to my mom. By the time Jonah's dad arrived to pick him up, Jonah and Mom had bonded over photos and talked about memories, and somehow things had shifted.

I couldn't be happier when Jonah's dad was chatting out on the porch for half an hour, despite turning down an invitation to come in by saying he wouldn't stay long. Seemed he had a lot to say about everything, and my mom wasn't shy on debating the merits of caffeine over decaf.

They both thought that decaf was the work of the devil.

At least, that is the part I heard—the rest was lost in the fact that Jonah and I found a quiet corner and spent the entire time kissing.

I could get used to this.

OUR FIRST OFFICIAL DATE WAS MY CHOICE, AND I knew Jonah was regretting his suggestion that I decided where to go. Even taller in skates, he hadn't let go of the side of the rink yet, despite me offering a hand.

"I'm taller and bigger, and I will pull you down," he kept saying every time he ignored my outstretched hand.

"Just one lap, and then pizza," I said for the tenth time, grinning at him and darting closer to steal kisses. The rink was quiet tonight, closed to the public, two-thirds cordoned off for figure skaters, and the other third emptying after a toddler group had finished. All of the toddlers had trainers in the shape of teddies, and I could see Jonah eyeing one as if it might be a lifesaver. We'd only been allowed here because I knew the owner, who knew my mom, and we had exactly one hour to enjoy the empty space.

Well, empty if you didn't count the lone figure skater over on his side, working on jumps with a harness and a coach who did more barking than encouraging. I recognized Kenji Kelly immediately, not because hockey and figure skating cross, but because he looked a lot like my favorite figure skater, Olympian Nathan Chen. Of course, Kenji was the same age as me and Jonah, and only in-training, rather than on the circuit. We'd also connected at a skating club when I was about ten or so—at the height of my dad being an asshole—and he'd been kind to me. We followed each other on Instagram, and we'd exchanged DMs a few times. I waved at him, and he acknowledged me with a quick nod as he started a complicated sequence of movements. I skated closer to Jonah and leaned on the barrier, resting my hand on his, then unpeeling his fingers and lacing them with mine.

"I'm not scared," he lied.

I pushed my skate a little, so it nudged his, then I reached up and kissed him, cradled his face with my free hand and actually devoured his mouth in the middle of a skating rink. Or the edge, at least.

He relaxed against me, and I softly tugged him from the barrier, taking his weight into balance, and pushing off backward, him coming with me, chasing for a kiss. Before he realized he'd let go of the side, I had him in the middle of our small part, and then, he froze and gaped at me.

"And how do you think I'm going to get back?" he asked, tension in every line of him. He wobbled, which I countered, and then, he wobbled in the other direction, and I shifted to balance him out again.

"I'll help you. Hold my hands." He slid his free hand from my arm, down to hold on for dear life.

"Push forward," I instructed, as I began to skate backward, and he glided with me.

I wasn't going fast, but to listen to him grumping, you'd think I was trying to set land speed records. After a while, he stopped warning me he was going to hurt me and seemed to settle into the gentle circles. Every time we completed a small loop, I kissed him, and we slid, quite literally, into a sweet routine of skate and kiss, and by the tenth time, he was smiling and tried letting go of one hand. The disconnect didn't last long, but he whooped and hollered like he was winning gold. We'd stopped for a drink—bottles of water in my bag—and I glanced at the clock, seeing we had a couple of minutes left.

"One last go-around?" I asked.

He kissed the question right out of me. "On my own?" he asked, or rather told me, as he pushed away from the boards.

Only he pushed too hard, he wasn't fully upright, his center of balance was off, and he was so fast that when he fell over, he slid right under the small barrier and into the figure skaters' side of the rink. I couldn't get there in time, landing at his side in a few seconds, but Kenji had reached him first, stopping him from sliding any further, and offering him a hand up.

Between us, we got him standing, and despite the pinwheeling, he was finally up and steady.

"Sorry," I apologized to Kenji, who smiled at me as if nothing fazed him.

"It's all good," he murmured, then brushed off Jonah's jeans, which had shavings of ice on the butt. I wasn't so sure I wanted the cute-as-fuck Kenji anywhere near my boyfriend's butt, but what could I say. "First time?" he asked Jonah, who returned his smile.

"Is it that obvious?"

Was Jonah flirting with Kenji? I grasped Jonah's hand and kissed him right there and then, because there was no way I was losing the best thing ever to a cute and sexy figure skater, no matter how many jumps he could do.

"Kenji!" his coach yelled.

Kenji's smile dropped, and I swear his shoulders tensed, which surely wasn't a good look for someone who was aiming for fluid on the ice.

"Work calls," he said, and skated, swirled, and jumped away from us, Jonah staring after him.

"He's cute, right?" I asked Jonah when we reached the side.

"You think he's cute?" Jonah asked with a frown, and I thought I heard a hint of jealousy in his tone. I wanted to punch the air—Jonah wasn't interested in Kenji; he was interested in *me*.

"Well yes," I began, and he narrowed his eyes at me, "but not in a boyfriend-I-want-to-kiss-as-badly-as-I-want-to-kiss-you kind of way."

He gave me an upnod. "Same."

One more kiss just to seal that deal, and then, we were off the ice, back in street shoes, and heading for pizza.

"How was that for a first date?" I asked him over a slice of pepperoni.

He reached for my hand. "Terrifying, thrilling, and perfect, but it's my turn next and we're going to see a movie sitting down in safety. Agreed?"

I'd go anywhere he wanted. Do anything he wanted.

Like was rapidly turning to love.

Chapter Fifteen

Jonah

I TRIED. I REALLY DID. BUT GETTING THE GIRLS TO SIT still for me to finish their hair was impossible. Lana said she was old enough to do her braids by herself— I had serious doubts, but whatever—while Gemma demanded that I use just red and green barrettes. There were only three because the others had disappeared into a black hole in space or were under the fridge, which was the same thing—and Polly was too tired and cranky to let me try to tame her curls.

"Mom, I did my best," I said as I paraded the trio of girls into the kitchen where my parents were frantically getting food ready for the Christmas Eve party. Dad glanced over the shoulder of his white dress shirt—Mom had insisted everyone dress up because Soren and his fathers were coming, like Tennant and Jared were royalty of some sort—and his eyes went wide.

"Well now, those are quite the hairdos," Dad said, then nudged Mom in the side while she was trying to add tiny holly leaves to her triple layer cake. Each layer was a holiday color, red, green, and white, and the icing was that super sweet fluffy stuff she only made on special occasions. Like hockey royalty coming to eat tiny meatballs. Adults were super weird. "Why don't I finish icing the cake, and your mother can work on the girls' hair styles."

"If you reach for this cake once more, Terrence, I will not be responsible for the fate of your fingers," Mom snarled in warning. Dad and I exchanged looks. "Girls, let Dad do your hair. I need to finish this cake."

Three young misses began whining at the same time. Dad wiped his hands on the apron Mom was wearing over her pretty gold cocktail dress. I let him take the girls back upstairs, then slipped in beside my stressed mother. She gave me a smile, then blew a strand of blonde hair from her face.

"He so badly wants to write something goofy on top of this cake with my fancy fake holly leaves," she explained then let her head come to rest on my shoulder. "I refuse to have Soren and Tyler's families eat a cake with 'Don't get your tinsel in a tangle' on top of it. Imagine what his supervisor would say if he saw that."

"People would probably laugh. Mom, seriously, everyone coming tonight is just normal people, you know?"

"I know, but I want…" She paused, blew out a breath, then turned to face me. She had a smear of icing on her cheek. "I'm trying to make a good impression. I know that most of the kids that go to Chesterford are wealthier than we are, and I want them, and the people Dad and I work with, to see that even though we might not have mad cash to burn, we can still put on a fancy shindig."

"Well, that cake is the fanciest thing I've ever seen. So, you're already above and beyond."

She smiled at me so brightly it nearly blinded me. "Thank you, Jonah." She took a moment from holly leaf placement to adjust my tie. We'd been granted a blessing of not having to wear a jacket, but trousers, tie, and a dress shirt had been mandatory. "Now, can you go grab the good dishes out of the cupboard and put them out by the food on the dining room table?"

"Sure." I wiped her cheek with my thumb. She

rolled her eyes at the frosting on my finger, then got back to work, her shoulders a little less tense than before.

Carrying my grandmother's fine dishes to the table, I paused to listen to my dad arguing with Lana about wearing her new winter boots with her party dress. While they haggled it out, I moved around the table after placing the good dishes by the silverware and fancy plastic cups. Mom had been cooking for days. There were about a dozen casserole dishes sitting in warmer trays, all covered with foil to keep them warm. Swedish meatballs, macaroni and cheese, baked ziti, some sort of cheesy broccoli dish, Spanish rice, mixed veggies, creamed corn casserole, and a dish of what looked like stuffed cabbages. How Mom had gotten all of this made while working and taking care of us, I had no clue. No wonder she was frazzled. And that was just the entrees. There were pies in the fridge, and of course, the winter cake she was hurrying to finish.

The doorbell rang. Mom yelped in alarm. Gemma raced down the stairs with one side of her hair done and the other loose, Polly in close pursuit clutching a Raggedy Ann doll that had somehow lost its leg in a mysterious manner we'd never been able to fully flesh out. The suspects were Lana and Gemma, but that was all conjecture.

"Girls, get back up here!" Dad yelled.

"Yes, get back up here you dummies!" Lana screamed down as she glared at the younger girls as if she were the one in charge. Which, most times, she was.

"Don't call your sisters dummies!" Mom and Dad corrected in perfect unison. I stepped in front of Gemma, then pointed up the stairs.

"You're not the boss of me!" the six-year-old huffed before spinning on her bare heel—where her shoes were was a mystery—then stomped back to my dad. Polly grabbed my leg as I opened the door to see Soren, his dads, Milo, and Lottie, as well as Felix and his dad, and Tyler and Mrs. Corrigan. They all made smiley faces at Polly hiding behind me.

"Welcome to the madhouse, aka our home," I said, lifted Polly to my hip, and stood back to let them all enter. Cold wind filled with tiny flakes of snow blew in with Tyler as he slipped to the back of the pack to sneak in a kiss. To Polly's cheek.

"Jo-bah give me to Ty-nerd," she commanded.

As her lowly servant, I could do no less, so I handed her to Tyler. She had won him over the first time he'd visited, and she knew she had him wrapped around her pudgy little finger.

"Ty-nerd, that's fitting," Felix whispered, then gave Tyler a poke in the side. I glanced at the exchange but said nothing as I gauged Tyler's reaction. He smiled and stuck his tongue out at Felix before giving me a warm look. My protective urges calmed.

"You look nice," I told Tyler as folks removed their snowy coats. The bell rang again. "I'm the doorman. The last time we had a party, Gemma snuck to the front door before we could get to it and told the new pastor of our church that Lana was a demon for taking the last lemon cookie and could he please send her to Hell."

Soren's dads laughed out loud. "That sounds just like something Lottie would say about her big brothers," Jared said.

"Yeah, that's true," Soren chuckled.

Dad jogged down the stairs, Lana behind him, and led our guests into our humble home. Tyler gave me a wide smile, then toted Polly into the living room as I opened the door to welcome Dad's co-worker Steve and his wife. My job as doorman lasted a steady thirty minutes or so, and by the time all the guests had arrived, you could barely move in our house. The girls were charming the pants off everyone—Lana explaining how our tree was a good one because, when we'd picked it, we'd found a bird nest in the boughs.

I slid up beside Tyler, glad to see he was at ease as he sipped the pink punch for those of us under twenty-one. His green eyes lit up when he looked to the side to see me there.

"Hey," he said as another Christmas song blared from the stereo. Soren and Felix joined us in the corner by the lucky bird nest pine tree decorated with only handmade ornaments made by us kids over the years and twinkly white lights. The glitter star I'd made in kindergarten sat at the very top, appearing a little worn, but still glittery. "This is a great party."

"I'm glad. Mom has worked her backside off." I nodded at Soren and Felix. They were holding hands. "We can go to my room after we eat to hang out. The girls will be going to bed soon, and it will be the adults down here. I have *Rocket League*. We can play that while we wait for the parental units to stop talking about taxes and the price of food."

"Sounds great." Soren smiled, then peeked over to his boyfriend.

"Yeah, I love *Rocket League*," Felix piped up.

Tyler gave me a sideways nudge, his gaze

glowing, and I had to give him a fast peck on the cheek. Mom called out that the food was now ready. We moved to get in line, the girls scurrying in front of me as they always did. I hoisted Polly to my hip so that she could tell me what she wanted, while Mom and Dad dished up food for the other girls. Polly wanted mac and cheese. That was all. She was growing tired, and so she got kind of upset there were no hot dogs to go with her mac and cheese. One simply did not serve mac and cheese and not have hot dogs to go with them. Silly Mom.

"I can nuke you one. Would that be okay?" I asked, and she nodded, then tucked her head into my neck. I left the line, carrying my sister into the kitchen, where I sat her in her booster, buckled her in, then hustled around to microwave a hot dog. She was waiting for me to cut it up when it was done, so I did that for her, then I sat down to supervise her eating.

"Did I nuke that wiener good?" I asked. She gave me a thumbs up, her cheeks filled with food. "Make sure you chew that." I looked up to see Tyler—who had two plates—Soren, and Felix all filing into the kitchen with their food in hand. "You guys can eat in the living room," I told them as they pulled out chairs. Tyler placed a dish loaded with piles of every offering in front of me.

"We're good to eat in here," Soren said as he lowered himself down to Dad's chair, then tucked a paper napkin over and behind his dark blue tie. "Dad is talking about retirement accounts or something, and Mr. Pike from your dad's office was asking me why young folks are making such a ruckus about climate change."

We all groaned, even Polly, who had no idea what climate change was yet.

"Yeah, he's like the head of the permit office or something? Dude is like a thousand years old. The last time I saw him he asked me if I really thought we needed charging stations for electric cars at our city parks."

"Man, old people." Felix sighed.

"Old people." Polly sighed as well.

We all chuckled, then ate. It was nice. Felix was being okay, a little odd, but then again, I was feeling a little odd around him, so it was probably a mutual oddness thing. Mom entered the kitchen with slices of cake for everyone, smiling at us as she served dessert. Polly ate all of hers, then fell asleep in her booster, her face smeared with ketchup and frosting.

"Let me get her to bed. You guys can chill in my room," I said, then unbuckled and lifted Polly up and into my arms. The guys followed, carrying cans of soda, and turned into my room as I made the left to get my sister ready for bed. We washed her face, changed her into her jammies, and I tucked her in with a kiss to her brow.

"Jo-bah read," she asked around a yawn.

"I have friends waiting for me, Pol," I explained. Her lower lip wobbled. "Okay, no tears." I grabbed a book from the stack we'd borrowed from the public library, a story about a penguin who wanted to learn to tap dance. Then I sat down beside her on the skinny toddler bed that had been handed down about four times now and started reading, only pausing at the sound of someone at the door.

Tyler smiled at me. "I love that story. Can I listen?" he asked.

Polly nodded with gusto, then told Tyler exactly where to sit. She was kind of bossy. Tyler sat on the floor, his eyes round and bright and resting on me as I read. Polly didn't make it past the third page. I turned off her lamp, flicked the nightlight on, and tugged Tyler to his feet.

"Time to kick Felix's butt in auto soccer," I whispered beside his ear. He nodded, kissed me quickly, and followed me into the hallway. The other girls were being led up the stairs as the sound of adult conversation and old Christmas songs floated upward.

Mom gave us a tired, but happy smile as she herded two exhausted girls to their room.

"Thank you for tucking in Polly," Mom said as the girls mumbled sleepily at her sides. "You are a great big brother." She patted my cheek, then got the girls moving once more.

"You really are a good big brother," Tyler said as we lingered in the hall for a minute, his fingers finding, then threading with mine. "I wish I had siblings."

"You say that now. When you wake up to discover that your term paper was used for confetti for Barbie and Ken's wedding, you'll be glad you're an only child," I tossed out, getting a snort of amusement from him. "Besides, your mom and Felix's dad are looking pretty close. You might get a new stepbrother someday."

"That would be really… weird," he whispered.

Yeah, it would be for sure. But hey, stranger things have and could happen. Like Tyler being my boyfriend.

Not that it was official or anything, but if Santa did bring me what I asked for, which was a new hoodie, I hoped he would also toss in having a boyfriend as a bonus gift.

"I really love being your boyfriend," Tyler

whispered before rising on his toes to kiss me on the lips.

Oh, wow, well okay then. *Thanks Santa!*

"I love being your boyfriend, too," I replied softly.

"Hey, are you ready for me to kick your butt?" Felix called from my room.

I was ready to kick *his* butt.

No one was ready for Tyler to be the grand champion.

Guess it was a night for all kinds of unexpected gifts.

Chapter Sixteen

Tyler

CHRISTMAS MORNING WAS ALL ABOUT PANCAKES AND bacon, and not just any old pancakes, but ones with smiley faces made from chocolate chips, and not just any old bacon, but crispy strips, and so much of it that we never ate it all. It was a tradition we'd started seven years ago, the first Christmas after Dad had gone, and we hadn't broken it since.

Only this year was different—James would be arriving as Mom was serving up the best bacon ever, and of course, Felix would be in tow. Mom and I had talked long and hard about James and his son being part of our tradition, and as much as I wanted to keep this space for me, I'd never seen Mom so happy. She was floating, doing her best Mariah Carey as she bustled around the kitchen singing, pressing a kiss to my head every time she passed. She and James had been an official thing since last night apparently, or so she said when she sat me down to tell me at breakfast. I'd known the news was going to be something that impacted my life when she didn't care how many Christmas chocolates I ate as we talked.

James Maxwell-Sinclair was officially her boyfriend now, smooching and everything, which made Felix my brother from another mother... and father...

Who knows...

Stranger things have happened.

I pulled out my cell, scrolling back through the messages I'd gotten this morning from Jonah, the first of which was the word *HELP*. He'd sent it at the ass crack of dawn, bleary-eyed, his hair hidden under a Santa hat, surrounded by gifts, wrapping paper, and three hyper excited girls.

I re-read the whole load of messages that had come in before I'd even opened my eyes, a story about Polly and a book, or Gemma and a doll, or Lana and a painting set, and the fact his parents had gotten him a hoodie. He sent a photo of himself in said hoodie, looking gorgeous, and I saved that photo to my all-things-awesome folder on my phone.

But it was the last message I was fixed on.

Jonah - *Merry Christmas, boyfriend.*

So, I sent him one straight back with an attached photo of me blowing him a kiss.

Tyler - *Merry Christmas, boyfriend.*

I'd watched the dots as they danced on the screen, and then, a small video came through, and I opened it eagerly. It was Jonah capturing the kiss and making a show of putting it in the pocket of his new hoodie.

"That's cute," Mom said over my shoulder, and I jumped a mile.

"Moooom," I whined because that was what was expected of me, given my mom was in my personal space watching videos sent to me, but it wasn't from the heart. "He is cute, isn't he." I said instead.

"I like him. I mean…" She stopped moving around and took the stool opposite me, a smudge of flour on her cheek caught my eye, but it was the sparkle in her eyes that held me. "I didn't want to like him, but he has this way about him, vulnerable, but confident, quiet, but somehow with important things to say. So yes, as long as he…"

Looks after you. Doesn't treat you badly. Isn't like your dad…

I could read all of that in her unfinished sentence.

"He's a gentle giant," I summarized.

She nodded, and startled when the doorbell sounded, abruptly flustered. "Do I look okay?"

The traditional pancake breakfast was always eaten while wearing traditional PJs, and just because this year we had guests, didn't mean things were going to be different. Mom's had kittens in Santa hats, mine was a superhero/drag race/Christmas homage that Mom had made for me last year.

"Flour, face," I said, and she checked her face in the mirror quickly, then went dead still, tracing where the flour had been. I was at her side in an instant, memories of other times when I would find her staring at her reflection and tracing a new bruise that hadn't been there before.

"Mom?" I deliberately moved between her and the mirror, breaking the connection with her past, and she started and blinked back to now, and smiled at me.

"Sorry, sweetheart."

I pressed a kiss to her heart, a throwback to when I used to check her heart rate to make sure she was okay—it wasn't as if I could do anything else for her when my dad lost his temper. He was a big man, and I was nothing to him but a fly he could swat out of the way of getting to Mom. Thank god he was gone.

"Am I doing the right thing?" she asked me, her eyes suddenly bright with emotion. "We have the house back, should I take some time to be me, or am I..." she threw me a tremulous smile. "Should I be happy?"

"Mom, of course you should. And I like James." I began, and then, smiled back at her, copying her words from earlier, changing a few words here and there. "I didn't want to like him, but he has this way about him, bad at board games, but thoughtful when he talks to you, quiet because he can't get a word in edgeways with Felix, but somehow, when he does talk, he makes me like him even more. So yes, as long as he..."

Looks after you. Doesn't treat you badly. Isn't like Dad...

She cradled my face, kissed my forehead, and hugged me close. "Thank you, Tyler."

Now, I was confused—hadn't we just exchanged mutual likes for our respective partners? There was nothing to thank me for. "What for?"

"For being the best son I could have wished for, and never giving up on me."

We hugged fiercely, all those memories between us would never leave, but it had made us stronger.

The doorbell sounded again, and I took my mom's hand and tugged her down the hallway, opening the front door with a flourish.

James and Felix were there, carrying boxes of things, both in big coats, snow swirling around them, and we hurried them inside. It was a shame they couldn't be in PJs as well, but that was too much to ask, given they'd braved snow to get here.

"Nice PJs," Felix said, and I eyed him with distrust. That was, until he peeled off his coat to reveal his own PJs, which he smoothed down with hesitance. "Dad said you do this," he murmured. "They're a bit short and tight, but it was all I had, and—"

"Dude!" I exclaimed and he winced. "Are those Power Rangers PJs?!"

He tipped his chin. "Yeah, and?"

"Favorite Power Ranger," I snapped out. "And don't say red, because everyone says red."

He blinked at me, then gave me a sly grin. "Tommy."

I gasped. "No way."

"Yes way, because as the Green Dragon Ranger,

he broke free of his brainwashing and decided to fight for good."

Now that deserved a fist bump.

Who would have thought Felix I shared a favorite Power Ranger.

BREAKFAST OVER, WE OPENED PRESENTS—THE merged collection of gifts a hodgepodge of paper and wrapping skills—clearly James and/or Felix were not imbued with the design gene, or at least not compared to me and Mom, who had been known to take all evening to wrap a single present with layers of tissue paper, drawn pictures, and handwritten notes. There was the usual stuff, like gift sets and books, but the present I loved the most was the one that James gave Mom.

It was an empty journal, leather-bound, with a gold filigree design. There was one word on the cover, *Beginning*, and I didn't have any idea of the significance of the word, but Mom started to cry, James gathered her into a hug, and they kissed, and that was Felix's and my cue to head out to the kitchen with our haul of chocolate.

"Seems like they might be serious," Felix said

around a mouthful of Lindt chocolate bitten from the biggest bar I'd ever seen.

I picked through my stash and pulled out my favorite Cadbury Dairy Milk that I knew Mom had ordered through an English friend to get the real stuff.

"I think so, yeah."

"Has your mom said anything about Dad?"

I countered, "Has your dad said anything about Mom?"

I sucked on the chocolate in my mouth and waited for him to counter again.

"He said she's special, and he asked me what I thought about her."

"Yeah? And what do you think?"

Felix raised an eyebrow. "I said that I'd be okay with it if my future step-brother shared his chocolate stash." He leaned to grab some of my stash, but I was as fast off the ice as I was on, and I beat him to it.

"And I said to Mom, I'd be cool with everything if my future step-brother didn't steal my stuff."

Then, we grinned at each other. It was just like the journal said.

It was a beginning.

. . .

I MISSED JONAH LIKE NOTHING ELSE, WHICH IS WHY, when the doorbell rang late Christmas afternoon, I was first to the door, hoping that, somehow, our day apart wasn't actually going to be spent apart at all.

I threw open the door, smile already there. Except it wasn't Jonah.

It was a man I never wanted to see again. Dad.

He was swamped in his big winter coat. I remembered him being taller, intimidating, blustering, with a cockiness that wooed clients to his real estate business, and that had somehow won over my mom when they were young.

"Tyler!" he said and smiled, but I noticed the smile didn't reach his eyes. It curved his lips, but it was as if he'd practiced how he was going to react. "Merry Christmas, Son." He added, then held out a badly wrapped gift. When he moved closer, my chest tightened, even more so when I smelled the alcohol on him.

"Who is it, Ty?" Mom called from inside, and there was the sound of talking I recognized as James, and then Felix.

"No one," I called back.

Dad stiffened at the barb. "I wanted to see you today," he said and waggled the gift. Some of the paper had come loose, but I didn't need to see the label to know it was a bottle of vodka.

"I'm fifteen," I said and pointed at the contents.

He seemed confused and exhausted, but there was nothing in my heart I could find to say to him. I didn't want him here, but I was frozen.

"Who did that to your hair?" Dad asked, and I almost reached up to touch the deep pink I had going on. "I hope you can get a refund," he laughed, and I think he was trying to make a joke. "You haven't grown much," he added. "Still, itty bitty Tyler. All pink and still gay? Here, take your present."

Fuck you! I didn't say that out loud, but all the slurs and the names and the pointed comments flew back at me.

Felix pressed a hand to my shoulder, and it startled me because I hadn't heard him step up to me. "The 'rents sent me to find out what's going on," he murmured. My dad frowned, all pretense at being kind slipping away. He moved closer, and I took a step back, right into Felix, who steadied me. "Everything okay here?" Felix asked.

"Who's this?" Dad asked, his voice slurring, pointing at Felix.

Felix ignored him. I ignored him. "What do you want me to do?" Felix murmured.

"Call 911," I said with all the calm I could muster, staring Dad right in the face. "There's a restraining order on William Alexander Corrigan, and he's on our property."

Felix immediately did what he was asked, and he didn't move an inch from my back as he connected to the cops.

"What the fuck you do that for?" Dad went for hurt, but he wasn't the gaslighting expert he thought he was, and his wounded expression wasn't moving me for an instant. "I'm your father. It's Christmas. I just want to see you, and I have a right to—"

"You have no rights!" Mom flew past me—god she was fast—James was right on her tail trying to catch her. Dad stumbled back, the present falling and smashing on the ground as Mom rounded on him. "Call 911!" she shouted back.

"Already done, and I'm leaving the line open," Felix replied, then tipped his phone. "And recording everything."

There was a face-off, James was right behind Mom, and Mom was way too close to my dad, whose demeanor changed in an instant.

"Who the fuck is this?" he shouted right in her face, and she winced, but didn't back down, and James stepped out to stand by her side. "You moved into my house?" Dad said, confused, slurring, and swaying on our pathway. It was cold—it hit me that all four of us, still in PJs and just socks, were standing in the snow with an icy breeze making flakes swirl from the trees lining the path. I shivered, Felix rubbed my arm and tugged me back to the house, but I stopped him, yanking myself free.

"I'm not leaving my mom alone with him!" I yelled at Felix, who immediately backed down, but stayed right by my side.

"My dad is there," Felix murmured. "I'm here."

My chest was so tight I thought that the panic might overwhelm me, but then, I heard sirens, and saw a car sweeping into our drive, flashing lights, and two cops. Everything was a blur. They carted dad off, as he screamed obscenities, laughing, then crying, and the remains of the vodka still lay outside. I padded into the kitchen, grabbed the dustpan, and went back to clear the glass, but Felix, who still hadn't left my side, took it from me and got any shards into a bag for disposal.

Mom hugged me. James hugged Mom. We sat in the kitchen with hot chocolate, me and Mom holding hands. Then it was James she held on to as well, even as she hugged me.

I unpeeled my fingers, shooing her away. "Get the hugs, Mom," I said with a smile.

She reached for me. "Are you okay?"

I nodded, then concentrated on breaking pieces of Dairy Milk into my hot chocolate, poking at them with my spoon. Felix copied, and I didn't tell him he couldn't have my candy. Why would that asshole of a dad come and ruin our perfect day? Why would he do this to us? Felix was messaging someone—probably Soren—and I was ashamed that, maybe, he was spreading around what happened, but he abruptly squeezed my hand, then tugged me out of the kitchen, gripping the top of my PJs and dragging me down the hall to the door. He flung it open, and I winced, expecting Dad, expecting danger.

But it was Jonah, with his mom, dad, and the girls, with boxes and smiles. Jonah immediately put his box down, which was full of food, and stood in front of me.

"Felix called me," he said.

"We wanted to be here for you and your mom." Jonah's mom sounded unsure.

"She'll love that; she needs that; she... the house is too..." I wasn't making any sense. Everyone moved in and the door closed, the cold locked outside.

Then, I was in Jonah's arms.

And it was everything.

Chapter Seventeen

Jonah

SOMETIMES, IT TAKES A REAL KICK IN THE ASS TO make you realize just how much you have, even if you don't have as much as others.

Like, I knew my family was okay. Sure, my mom was a bit nerdy over all things Bowie, and Dad had this embarrassing thing where he broke out his Run DMC song collection at the drop of a hat, and yeah, my sisters could be loud at times, but overall, they were okay.

Then, you ran face first into a situation like Tyler had faced on Christmas Day with his no-good father, and you *really* realized just how much you have. No, we were not rich or famous—yet, because I had plans

—but we had love. There were no issues with any kind of dependency in our home—no abuse, no abandonment, no violence like so many other kids dealt with on the daily.

Maybe my shoes weren't the newest or my gaming console the shiniest, but, man, was I ever thankful for the solid family unit I had. Seeing that upheaval a few days ago had hit me hard. I'd spent as much time as possible with Tyler to try to counteract the darkness that had arrived on his stoop. He seemed to be lighter now, four days after Christmas, as we hopped on a city bus to meet the guys at a nearby theater that showed only retro flicks to watch *Die Hard* on the big screen.

"Did you see this?" Tyler asked as we rode along, the bus packed with weary people on their way home from a long day at work. We still had another ten days off school and had plans for every day. It was overwhelming at times—in the best way possible—to have so many friends. I'd never had this kind of friend group before, and it made me feel like I might be a good person deep down to see my friends and followers climbing steadily. Not that you should base how decent a person you are on social media, my mom was always telling me, but I was fifteen, and what my peers thought of me *was* important. I leaned over to see what had his attention. "Soren just dropped this in the team chat. Seems his dad is setting up some sort of skate for the guys at the new Railers training facility in Dauphin. It's going to be Ten and Dieter Lehmann for a day. Hey, we should tag Kenji Kelly. I bet Trent will be there too. He's always where his husband is when he's not at Rainbow Skate."

"Oh sure, yeah, go ahead and tag Kenji. He's cool," I said, making a mental note of the day and time of this skate session with the Coyotes. "It's pretty awesome of Ten and Dieter to do that for the team."

"Yeah, Soren is saying that his dads are trying to get him out away from his stream." Tyler grinned over at me just as a man behind us coughed up a lung or something.

I winced at the sound. Tyler could have ridden over with Felix, but he had insisted on coming on the bus with me. Mom and Dad were rationing gas right now—the bills for Christmas were about to drop—so it was public transportation for me. Tyler coming along was just… well, it was typical Tyler. Sweet and considerate.

"He *has* been streaming non-stop over break," I conceded as the bus slowed at our stop. I stood up, offered Tyler my hand, and got all toasty warm inside when he took it. Tiny sparks danced up my arm right to my gut. The urge to kiss him was strong, but I'd been working on a cold for a few days, nothing serious, but sniffles, and didn't want to infect Tyler like my sister Lana had infected me. Kids were so germy.

"Yeah, but he got *Leagues of Battle Knights* for Christmas, so they should have expected him to stream that hard."

We exited the bus, ignoring the unhappy looks from a few old people. Maybe they were upset at us being a biracial couple, or that we were two guys holding hands, or that Tyler had pink hair and eyeliner, or that I was wearing green. Who knew, and who the hell cared. Not me. Crusty old farts could glower at us all they wanted. I was proud to be twice the bi.

The old theater was tucked into a strip mall. We jogged across the parking lot, the cold end-of-the-year wind rough on our cheeks as tiny bits of ice scoured our faces. Tyler bounced off me a few times, his shorter legs tangling him up as I pulled him at top speed. We were laughing hard when we burst into the theater lobby, the warm smell of freshly popped popcorn greeting us. Our gang waited for us at the doors of the one and only theater, hands filled with soda, candy, and tubs of buttery popcorn.

"We were about to send out some bloodhounds," Soren called as Felix sprinkled garlic powder and salt on his popcorn. "Felix, man, I am so not kissing you now."

"Have some then," Felix said, dousing his boyfriend's corn with garlic. "Now we both have troll breath."

"If I have to sit next to two trolls making out, I'm going to move to another row," Shaun said, nudging Soren in the side as Felix comically puckered up at his boyfriend. The other guys all joined in on riding Soren about his garlic troll boyfriend as I stepped up to the register and pulled out my wallet.

"Two please," I said, then heard Tyler stepping up beside me. I glanced down at him. "I got this," I said firmly before he could offer. "This was my idea. I asked you out. I'm paying."

"Okay, then I get the snacks." He was pretty set about that; I could tell by the way he replied.

"Cool." I bought our tickets, got my tub of corn and a large Coke, then stopped at the popcorn dressing stand to shake some pepper and grated cheese on my popcorn. Tyler added a sprinkle of ranch topping to his.

We filed into the rundown theater as a pack, fourteen teenage boys in JV jackets—well thirteen in JV jackets, as I didn't have one—then found our seats. The place was pretty much deserted, and so we spread out a bit, tossed our feet to the seats in front of us, and began shooting the shit as some old ass trailers from a hundred years ago played on the dusty screen. Movies like *Escape from New York*, *48 Hours*, and the first *Top Gun* set the mood. A few popcorn battles broke out before the movie we had come to see began.

Since we had the theater to ourselves—who other than bored teenaged guys would go out in a sleet and snow storm to eat junk food and jeer at Hans Gruber—we kind of let loose. So much so that the old guy who sold popcorn had to come in with his flashlight and cane to tell us to shut the hell up or we'd get kicked out and miss the ending. Like we didn't know how this movie ended.

We did settle down after the warning though. Felix and Soren had taken a couple's seat behind the pack and started making out.

I slid my arm around Tyler's shoulder, using my left hand to cram popcorn into my face while John McClane was rubbing his bare toes in the carpet. Even with the sound up as loud as it was, it was hard to ignore the two guys going at each other like rabid zombies in the row behind us. Shaun, being the captain, finally turned to face Soren and Felix.

"You two think you can calm the hell down a little?" he asked as he gave the two breathless guys his best serious captain face. "If I wanted to hear that, I would have stayed home with porn and tugged one off."

"Sorry," Soren whispered as Felix slunk down in his seat.

Tyler and I exchanged an uncomfortable look. We, then, stared at the screen without saying anything about the heavy petting that had taken place right behind us. I had no clue how far Soren and Felix had gone, and I didn't want to know, but it was obvious they were for sure closer to doing *it* than Tyler and I were. I wasn't sure how to bring up sex and all of that to Tyler, or if I was ready to go further than kissing. Right now, I was happy to kiss on him and hold him, but what if he wanted more? I peeked to the side. His gaze met mine.

"I'm not in a hurry to do anything," he whispered into my ear, then pressed a kiss right under it. That warm slippery kiss made me instantly hard, so I shifted my popcorn tub around a bit, smiled back at him, and nodded.

"I'm not either," I confessed before pecking his cheek. We nestled in as close as we could get, my arm on his shoulder, his head on mine, and spent the next couple of hours yelling quotes at the screen at the same time Bruce Willis said them.

It was the best time out with friends that I could ever recall. And that counted my gang in my old school. The Coyotes were welcoming, fun, and cool as hell. There was no feeling odd about my darker skin, curly hair, or the fact I was holding hands with a femme guy as we raced out of the theater into a winter wonderland.

Our phones all came alive, worried parents asking when they could come pick us up because of snow. It was falling steadily, the flakes big as quarters, the kind of snow my father always said wouldn't last because only small flakes stuck. I was pretty sure that was BS Dad talk, but who knew. Maybe Dad was a secret snow meteorologist, but I suspected not.

"Guys, I live about two blocks from here," Shaun said as we huddled under the old marquee, hands cold, breath fogging in front of us. "My dad's away, and Mom will be cool with it, so why don't you all just text your parents and ask them if you can sleep over. This way, they can come get you tomorrow when the roads are plowed."

We all thought that sounded great. Mom wasn't keen on last-minute changes in plans, but also, not keen on driving to get me in a snow storm or leave me on a city bus with a driver that was in a hurry to get home before the snow got too deep.

Mom: *If I get a text from Shaun's mother saying it's okay, then okay with us. You don't have any clean underwear.*

I looked up from my mother's text to see the other guys all staring at their phones.

"My mom is worried about me not having clean underwear," I said, and everyone laughed and said, "Mine too!"

Fifteen minutes later, we were all at Shaun's house, a big split-level with a massive, finished basement his mom hurried to set up for the influx of hockey players. His mom was super pretty and made some killer nachos, plus his dad wasn't there, which meant we could relax away from hockey. We spread out on the floor, blankets and old sleeping bags, sodas all over, as well as bags of chips and cheesy puffs. Midnight came and went. We were all talking, joking, and eating as much junk as we could. It was perfect. And through it all, Tyler was curled up at my side, sharing kisses and Snickers, feeding me cold nachos.

When I finally dozed off around three in the

morning, I did so with Tyler's bubblegum-pink head on my chest. The other guys were out cold, a few snoring softly, a few others whispering in the dark as the muted lights from their phones lit their faces.

I'd never felt more accepted in my life, or more in love. I couldn't wait for school to start up again so that I could show off the new and improved Jonah Robinson. I hoped everyone liked him. I know I did.

Chapter Eighteen

Tyler

THE NEW RAILERS TRAINING FACILITY IN DAUPHIN was a temple to Railers hockey, and the most cutting edge thing I'd ever seen. Everything sparkled as new, silver, and the familiar dusky blue colors everywhere from the ice to the wall and into the locker rooms. Huge photos of the Railers' stars adorned the lobby, and it was weird to see Soren's dad standing right under his enormous photo. He looked so normal, in jeans and a Railers hoodie, but in the photo above, he was in the middle of shooting on goal and every line of him was perfect.

I will not crush on Soren's dad.

Everyone was just like me, church-quiet, soaking

in every little bit of this pristine place, and staring up at their favorite player, and for a moment, Ten, along with Railers D-Man Dieter Lehman, stared at us, arms folded across their chests. It didn't last long, because both men dropped the pretense at being in control of anything and ushered us through to the locker rooms. We scrambled to get to cubbies, and I was faster than Soren at getting to the space with his dad's name on it. I never knew that training facilities had named cubbies, but you bet I was going to steal my favorite player's space.

"Not cool, dude," Soren whined and threw puppy eyes at Ten, who was in deep conversation with Shaun.

"You snooze you lose," I deadpanned, and Soren laughed so loud that Ten came over to ask what was going on, which made me go scarlet, I was sure of it.

"My cubby," Soren pointed and pouted up at his dad.

"N'aw," Ten said and side-hugged his son. "I knew I was your favorite."

"Only because Shaun beat me to Adler's space," Soren said with a wink, which earned him a noogie, which was fun to watch because, jeez, his dad was strong.

We got dressed for this amazing training

experience—who else got to go out on actual NHL training ice. Not this guy, anyway.

"Have I said how much I love that your dad is Tennant Madsen-Rowe?" Felix sauntered over all kinds of casual, then sneaked a brief kiss with Soren.

I shoved at Felix. "No macking in the locker room!"

Felix snorted a laugh, Soren rolled his eyes, and they both pointed at Jonah, who was lurking by the door staring up at the logo of the Railers team and taking photos. When Soren suggested he come with us—the resident photographer for everything—I was way past excited that he would be here for what promised to be the most perfect morning ever. He'd also gotten permission to photograph both the professional players, with the proviso that they got to check the images first, but I knew every shot he captured would be perfect.

"Do you know why we're called the Harrisburg Railers?" Dieter asked Jonah, who jumped a mile because he'd been so focused on what he was doing. Shoulders back, he stood to attention, and I would have smiled, but he was wide-eyed. There was nothing scary about Dieter—he was big, yes, but he had a way about him that was gentle, even if he was a big hard defenseman.

"No, sir, I don't."

"Okay, you research that, then write me a two thousand word essay to be completed by the end of practice today."

Jonah's bottom lip fell. "Of course, sir."

Dieter nodded, then fake-punched Jonah's arm. "Kidding. We're called the Railers because Harrisburg was where the steel was produced for some of the first steel rails for the railroad." He pointed to his jersey with its train logo. "Cool, right?"

Jonah blinked up at Dieter, and his smile blossomed in front of my eyes. "So cool," he said, and I think I was witnessing the beginning of a serious case of hero worship. Now, if Dieter liked taking photographs as well, then…

"What's your name?" Dieter asked.

"Oh. Jonah, I'm Jonah."

Dieter held out a hand. "Dieter. Tell me about your camera."

I smiled as I watched Jonah and Dieter chatting about cameras and film and dark rooms. I had an errant thought that maybe I needed to visit Jonah in a dark room. Surely, dark rooms made for good private kissing. Great. Now, I'm thinking about kissing.

"Eyes on your skates, Tyler!" Shaun snapped at me, super tense as he had been all morning.

"Sorry, cap," I apologized, and retied my laces, because I'd done a piss poor job of that while staring at a smiling Jonah. We headed for the ice, the door slamming open behind us and a windswept Kenji Kelly stumbling in—seemed, maybe, he saved all his grace for the ice—apologizing for being late.

"What's *he* doing here?" Shaun muttered.

"I asked him," I semi-apologized. "I thought maybe Dieter would have brought his husband with him." Shaun blinked at me. "Y'know, Trent Hansen, the figure skater, and Kenji is a figure skater." I pointed at Kenji, and it happened that he caught me, grinning a hello until his gaze rested on Shaun, and his smile fell. "Stop scaring him!" I warned Shaun out of the corner of my mouth.

Shaun turned away from me, heading past each cubby, a terse comment here and there, and nothing at all like what he was normally like. I guess the pressure of being there with NHL stars, when everyone said he could be one of them, was heavy.

We headed out to the ice, and took a moment to take it all in. The boarded oval didn't have much in the way of seating to watch—that wasn't the point of this place, it was the single point where Railers skaters learned how to be a team, and we had two of the best on the team waiting on the ice for us.

"Holy shit," Shaun broke the silence, and sounded a lot less tense than he had before. "Holy fucking shit, this is everything."

He was allowed to say that. We stayed quiet and let him have his moment.

"Fuck," he repeated, and when Ten noticed us all gathered by the gate, waiting to come out, he skated over, and Shaun's entire posture changed from shock and awe, to respectful and excited. His emotions were infectious as Ten iced to a stop with the biggest grin.

"Let's do this!" he said, as Dieter skated up next to him.

"Ready, guys?" Dieter asked.

We chorused a *yes* to both, and in my periphery, I clocked Jonah buzzing around capturing the whole thing on camera.

Only a tiny part of me was nervous about hitting the ice with him watching; the rest of me was proud, and yes, I definitely showed off when he was watching. I may not be the biggest player, or the most physical, but I was fast, and Jonah loved that.

He told me so.

In Shaun's basement.

In fact, he spoke for so long that night about how I looked on the ice, that Felix had to tell him to shut up.

Soren fist bumped Ten as he skated past, wriggling as Ten caught him in a hug and smooshed his face with his glove.

"… hate you!" Soren said, but he was grinning like a loon when Ten let him go.

"Okay, boys, line up at center."

We all skated straight to the middle, and just after we were all lined up, a flash of scarlet and silver announced the arrival of Kenji, who spun and slotted nicely at the end, a grin on his face and a fist bump for me. It didn't escape my notice that Shaun frowned at Kenji—probably didn't see a place for a figure skater on hockey ice—but he had his idol in the shape of Ten, so the frown didn't last long.

"Do you think Trent is here somewhere?" Kenji asked, a little breathless with excitement. "I have so much I want to ask him."

"I know he's here. I saw him," Felix said from my other side. "He was Facetiming someone."

"Oh my god, oh my god," Kenji said, and he almost hopped from skate to skate. I glanced down—he was wearing hockey skates, not the ice skates I expected.

"Can you play hockey?" I asked, not expecting him to be on the ice for actual skating with us.

"Sure, I can, just don't like it as much as figure skating."

"Just don't break anything; not on my watch."

"Can I ask you something?" He pointed at my hair. "Is that shade 403 pink quartz, or the 404?"

"Oh, 403, but I tend to—"

"Shut it," Shaun snapped from down the line, and I mimed zipping my lips, then turned to Kenji and mouthed "later."

"Okay, guys." Dieter did a head count. "There's twenty-one of you, so split up into threes, and we'll work on some..." His voice was lost in the melee of us grabbing friends, and I happily let myself be dragged into the Soren/Felix show. It amused me that Shaun ended up with Kenji in his three, after Kenji skated to his side. Shaun eyed him with confusion, and I saw him raise a hand to ask Ten for help, but he dropped it quickly when Kenji stared up at him with his best anime wide-eyed pout. It didn't help that Shaun was over average height, already up there and over six-foot in his skates, whereas Kenji was like me, slight and pocket-sized, although he was not rocking the pink like I was.

We hustled up and down the ice, taking shots on goal, just enjoying every second of the feel of skating on the pristine—professional—ice, stopping for Railers-endorsed energy drinks, then laughing at Ten as he tried to pirouette with Trent, who'd joined us on the ice. Trent was a former Olympic skater, but there was nothing *former* about his moves. I couldn't wait for Kenji to connect with him, only for some reason, Kenji was switching between heading for Trent, and hiding behind Shaun. Something was wrong there, but I was having way too much fun to analyze Kenji's shyness. Soren, Felix, and I were, by far, the best line out there. Well, I thought we were, but when it came to the end of the messing about, and we got serious—or as serious as we could get as enthusiastic school skaters—it was Shaun with Kenji and a bemused Gavin Neely who seemed to be the most connected. Like me, Kenji was fast across the ice, and even though he was a figure skater, he also had some hockey moves, which involved puck handling and skating fast to avoid everyone else—pretty much the same as me.

In hindsight, it was mostly Shaun who carried that line, and none of us were surprised when he got the man-of-the-messing-around-with-NHL-stars award. Ten had spent some time with him, chatting, working on his corner work, and I was pleased for Shaun. He worked hard and deserved everything that he got.

Jonah leaned over the boards, his elbows resting

on the side, and I caught drive-by kisses as I skated lazy laps to cool down, then came to a stop in front of him. His camera was up, and he caught a series of action shots as I drew closer, and then, a final one of me right up in his face.

"You looked so sexy out there," he murmured and tugged me closer, which was easy given I was on skates, and then, kissed me soundly right there in the practice facility.

"Not as sexy as you taking photos."

Some ass sprayed to a stop next to me. "Now who's kissing when they shouldn't be!" Felix taunted and rubbed an icy glove in my face, which led to the epic training facility showdown that made the day the best of my entire life.

When we left, it was Jonah who spotted Kenji talking to Trent and taking a photo for posterity, but I didn't see one figure skater talking to another, but Trent talking and Kenji subdued and backing away with his arms crossed over his chest, defensive. I immediately went over, but Kenji must have sensed he had an audience because he nodded at Trent and then, left, his skates padding on the mat, disappearing into the locker room.

"Hey, are you friends with Kenji?" Trent asked, and I nodded. I didn't know him that well, but he was a nice guy, and I'd be glad to be his friend, if only to exchange tips on dye colors.

"Will you do me a big favor?"

I was suddenly shy of the Olympic champion asking me for a favor. "Sure."

Trent handed me a small card with a scribbled number on the back. "This is my personal cell, okay? But you can always get to me through Ten's boy, Soren, if you need me."

"Okay." This wasn't weird at all. I glanced down at the card with its brilliant rainbow on the other side.

"Promise me you'll… look… if he needs help…"

"With his skating?" I completed as a question.

"With anything. I'm going to look into some stuff, and I… just be a good friend, and keep that number."

"Sure."

Trent gave me a weak smile, then pointed at my hair. "403 quartz or 404?"

An Olympian was asking *me* about hair color? Best. Day. Of. My. Life.

Chapter Nineteen

Jonah

IT WAS FUNNY IN THAT ODD WAY, NOT THAT HA-HA way, how I suddenly looked forward to going back to school.

For the past few years, school had been a place I would have rather avoided, choosing to spend my time in the school paper's dark room, or slinking around taking shots of students living their high school dreams. My dreams had always been just making it through another day of being an outcast, or, and this was even worse, being a jerk to other people. Like other people had been to me, which was a totally fucked up way of coping with my differences.

Walking into Chesterford on the first day back

from winter break, I felt like a different man. And in many ways, I was. One of the best people on the planet had given me a chance at redemption. The same person who was now walking at my side, his fingers meshed with mine as he chatted animatedly with Soren, Felix, and Shaun. Tyler was super talkative today. I wasn't sure if he was happy to be back at school, or if it had something to do with Trent Hansen talking hair with him. He'd gushed about that for days and was still gushing.

People in the halls looked at me differently. Lots of them smiled, or waved, or nodded as I passed by with my posse. Oh man, I used the word posse. My father was rubbing off on me. It was like those commercials about turning into your parents, only I was living it. Next, I'd be breaking into the Tootsie Roll dance in American History class. Why were my folks so weird?

"Hey, we have practice today to get ready for the game with the Ephrata Gators on Thursday," Tyler said as Soren peeled off to find Chelsea for some gamer group thing. Felix and Shaun stopped at their lockers, leaving me and Tyler to make our way to homeroom. "If it's okay with your folks, my mom is going to pick us up at Hot Pot Noodle after our usual post-practice gluttony. You want to come? We can noodle-kiss again."

Like I would pass up another noodle-kiss? "Yeah, I'll meet you there. We have a newspaper meeting right after seventh period, which is gym for me, so I'll just shower, do the meeting, and then meet you at the rink?"

"You are the *perfect* boyfriend!" He rose to his toes, kissed me so hard my head swam, then jogged off to shove his hockey gear into his locker and head to homeroom. I watched him go, smiling at the spring in his step. Tyler seemed so much happier. Maybe, just maybe, I was a part of that glowing bounce he now had.

THE FIRST DAY BACK ENDED WITH ME RACING TO MR. Wheeler's room for a long, boring meeting after playing volleyball for forty minutes. My hair was still soaked from my shower, and my tie was in my back pocket. Good thing Mr. Wheeler was cool. He was a total bohemian dude forced to wear a tie all day long. Long hair, beard, totally into old classic rock, talked about getting stoned off his ass at a Peter Frampton concert back in the seventies. He was the campus hippie who was pretty cool with everything as long as it didn't harm anyone. Love and peace man. A lot of the kids made fun of him, but I liked him. He had a good eye for photography and a general dislike of "*The Man*," which made his employment by a private school all that more confusing.

"Gotta pay the bills, Jonah," he'd reply whenever I would ask him why he was here and not teaching classes at Bard, Mount Holly Oak, or Portland State U, the liberal colleges. "Besides, my partner works for the assistant governor, so Harrisburg adjacent it was. Also, I like the trees here."

Yeah, the campus had nice trees. Mr. Wheeler was right about that. It would be a few long, cold months before we could be outside during lunch enjoying the shade from those grand old oaks that gave Mr. Wheeler such pleasure.

After fielding about a dozen dumb story suggestions—did we really want to dig into yet another story about the cafeteria not offering gourmet nut choices with lunches? No, we did not, thanks Katie—Mr. Wheeler yawned, scratched his beard, then leveled looks at all of us.

"Okay, junior journalists and photojournalists, I need you to think harder about the world around you.

Are you kids telling me that your biggest concerns are the nut choices in the cafeteria or that the bathrooms should have a fragrance dispenser for every stall? I mean, where are your heart and soul concerns? What should Chesterford be doing to help battle climate change? How can the student body further the fight for human rights? Where are the electric car charging stations we were promised when the last school budget was passed?"

"Mr. Wheeler, the principal told us that we couldn't write about radical things, remember?" Katie said as she twirled a shank of red hair around her finger. We all nodded. The first edition of the *Chronicle* had gotten the principal worked right the hell up when we printed a story about the lack of diversity training for athletic coaches. Mr. Wheeler had been raked over the coals for that one, but he had stood by Katie's story.

"Yeah, well, the principal is an old fart." He stroked his gray beard as a wicked smile pulled at his lips. "And not a cool old fart like me. An uptight old fart. Fine, we'll go with lighter subjects, but I want each of you to write me an editorial about something important. More important than how to make friends, or what kind of pets you have, or the importance of not breaking curfew. Give me something with meat. Jonah, I want you to find something that's not so run-of-the-mill jock stuff. Yes, your boyfriend and the hockey team are dreamy." Everyone snickered. I blushed hotly. "And while your project about them is coming together well, I want you to stretch your wings. Look into something not hockey. Find something that has some real energy and use that camera to explore it. Maybe work with one of the staff writers to show us a side of Chesterford that we rarely see. There are places on campus that you kids would freaking love if you found them."

"But most of those off-limits places are off-limits," Katie said, looking at the other two kids who contributed to the paper, then to me. "Are you saying we should sneak into off-limits places for a story?"

"Of course not. I would never suggest any of my future journalists and photojournalists nose around in something that those in positions of authority dictate." With that he sat back, placed his hands on his little round tummy, and began humming some old stoner song by the Grateful Dead or... well, I didn't really know any other old stoner songs. We all stared at him openly. He sighed before sitting up to gaze at us with gray eyes. "Kids, go look for news. It's literally all around you. Don't settle for mediocrity. Snoop around, dig up facts, use those brilliant brains for something other than TikTok videos."

"But what kind of things should we snoop around *for*?" Katie asked and got a chuckle from our advisor.

"Put your noses to the ground, intrepid reporters. Go now. Make me proud. Go. Skedaddle. I have a roast at home waiting for me." He encouraged us out of his classroom, smiling and nodding at our questions. The door closed in our faces.

I looked at Katie, Earl, and Wanda in utter confusion. "Why can't old people just talk in normal-speak?"

They all shrugged, then slumped off, each of us trying to come up with an idea about something important, but nothing that would get us in trouble with the principal. When I stepped out of the high school, the hairs in my nose froze instantly. I jogged to the rink, not stopping once, until I burst through the doors to hear the sounds of the team on the ice. It wasn't much warmer in here, but there was no wind. I took my usual seat behind the bench, opened my English Lit book because Ms. Nachez-Peirce had hit us with an assignment due in a week. She wanted us to create a storyboard for one classic book from her chosen list. I mean, really? How the hell did you create a storyboard for *A Tale of Two Cities*, *The Color Purple*, or *Don Quixote*? Like, seriously, where did teachers get these ideas? Oh, and we were not allowed to use images from any movies based on the books. Thanks a ton, Ms. Nachez-Peirce.

It was hard to concentrate on anything with Tyler on the ice. I closed my laptop, grabbed my camera, and did what I was born to do, took pictures. English Lit work could wait until my boyfriend and I were in separate houses. I loved watching Tyler skate, and so by the time practice was over and we were hustling to Hot Pot Noodle Shop with the team, I'd done zero homework, but had taken about two hundred shots of the Coyotes, mostly Tyler, but some of the other guys too.

We burst into the noodle shop with hoots and sighs of appreciation for the warmth. Servers smiled at us, moving quickly to set up tables, the scrape of table legs and chairs battling with Drake. We all helped out, and soon we were diving into some delicious ramen. I fed Tyler and he fed me, both of us using our chopsticks, me dropping chicken on his lap. He jumped. We all laughed. And I got a kiss without noodles. An hour or two passed, everyone loud, the eatery bustling around us as customers came and went.

"Hey, man, it's after eight," Shaun said, holding up his phone to show us all. "We better head home and hit the books."

"Ugh, Shaun, you are *such* an old man!" Felix moaned, the rest of the team breaking into imitations of Old Shaun waving his cane in the air or complaining about being up past nine p.m. in a creaky, elderly voice.

"Hey, make fun if you want, but we all have to keep our grades up to stay on the team," he replied. "Also, please fuck all the way off."

He flipped the table off. Everyone howled in amusement, then, sadly the party began to break off as guys left one by one. Tyler and I were the only ones remaining, and after I called home, we bundled up to go wait outside for my mom to come get us. It was super cold outside, the wind snapping the Hot Pot Noodle sign back and forth, so we ducked around the corner. We'd been cuddling inside, but a table of kids and their parents had come in and we'd been getting some dark looks, so we took ourselves outside to kiss a little more. We'd keep each other warm.

The windbreak felt good. I slid an arm around Tyler,

cinching him close, hoping to get a good round of kissing and hugging in before my mom showed up. Pressing him to the wall, I lowered my lips to his throat, after moving his scarf out of the way, to nibble at his neck. That was when we both heard shouts flying by on the arctic winds.

Someone shouting for help. A guy.

"Did you hear that?" Tyler asked.

I nodded, grabbed my bag, and raced around the back of the shop, Tyler in hot pursuit. Two huge guys in Chesterford varsity jackets nearly bowled us over as they raced away into the night.

"Dudes, seriously?!" I barked as Tyler slammed into me.

"Don't hurt me!" a very familiar voice pleaded.

Tyler glanced at me eyes wide. "Was that Miles?"

"Yeah, I think so." My pulse spiked. What the hell was going on that had sent two linebackers running into the dark?

"Shit," Tyler said, threw his hockey bag down, yanked his stick out, and ran past me as I fumbled to get my camera lens cap off.

"Tyler, what the hell?!" I barked, dropping my lens cap into the slush. "Tyler! Hold up!" He was not listening. Off he sprinted like a jackrabbit as I slapped around in dirty snow and God knows what else—probably piss and dumpster juice—to find my lens cap. "Tyler!" I shouted, fingers finally latching onto the circlet of plastic. I shoved it into my pocket, uncaring what nastiness was dripping off it, and took off after my boyfriend. I could hear Tyler yelling as I came around the corner, my camera bouncing off my heaving chest. If he got hurt by whatever kind of predator was back here I was going to lose my shit.

"Get away from him!" Tyler yelled, his stick over his head, as I ran around another dumpster to find some skinny guy with lanky hair waving a knife at Miles. I took several images in rapid succession of the perp. Tyler brought his stick down on the guy's shoulder, hard, and the dude yelped in pain. The stick snapped in half with a crack. He spun to glare at us, saw two people witnessing his crime, and took off like a rabbit, the knife still in his hand.

"Oh shit, shit, shit," Miles panted, his eyes wide with fear, his hand gushing blood all over the place.

"Dude, you're bleeding," I said because I was that fucking brilliant.

"I know," Miles croaked as he slid down the wall to sit in an inch of fresh snow. Tyler knelt beside him, yanking his hand out to stare at the wound in the dim light of a lone lightbulb over the back door to the noodle shop kitchen, which closed tight to keep the cold out. This rear parking lot was a mugging just waiting to happen. No security lights to speak of, and lots of dark places for shifty sorts to lurk, and a wide-open space that led to a major highway to get away clean, like the dude who had just cut Miles had. I did have him on film though. Well, not film, but a memory card, which I would gladly hand over to the cops. "He jumped out of that stupid bush when I parked. The guys took off."

"This looks pretty deep," Tyler said as he held Miles' quaking hand. "I think it should get stitches. Jonah's mom is coming soon. Do you want us to take you to the hospital?"

"Why would you do that?" Miles asked as I dug out a clean hankie for him to tie around what was probably a defensive slash.

"Because we're not assholes like your stupid friends," Tyler replied. Miles pulled his hand free, then stood. He towered over Tyler, his hand wrapped in my fave blue Railers kerchief. I took a step to bar Miles from touching my boyfriend, the one who had saved his stupid ass.

"You two will always be assholes," he snarled, stalking off to climb into a sleek black sports car, his father's Bugatti, which I knew he was not old enough to drive. I'd like to see him explain all the blood over the fine leather seats to Daddy. Off he went into the night, peeling rubber, leaving us standing in the cold, minus one hankie and one hockey stick.

"That's gratitude for you," Tyler sighed, tossing the broken half of his stick into the dumpster.

"You can't fix stupid," I mumbled as I stared long and hard at the parking lot. Maybe *this* was something that could be used for an article for the school paper. Maybe I could petition someone in power—a congressman or a senator or the mayor—to install more lights here for the safety of their constituents. I wasn't sure if a senator would even talk to me as I wasn't old enough to vote, but it was worth a try.

"No, but you can save stupid from being mugged," Tyler replied as a flash of headlights swept over us. I recognized my mom's car right off. "Maybe he'll be less of a jerk to us from now on."

"Maybe." I took his hand, saw it was covered in Miles' blood, and gave him a big grimace. "Your mom will freak out when she hears about this."

"Yeah, probably, but man, did we snap into action huh?" He wiped his hand on his jeans, but I was pretty sure his mom was going to freak out in a major way despite the swipe of palm on denim. "Guess we're sort of like paladins or knights out saving the common folk from villainy."

I pecked his cheek as my mother rolled up beside

us, then rolled her window down. David Bowie's "Heroes" floated out into the cold air.

Huh, I guess my guy and I *were* champions. I'd never have thought it was possible for me to be this proud, this happy, this whole.

It's amazing what love can do.

Epilogue

Tyler

WE COULD NEVER HAVE REALIZED THAT HANDING IN the recording would cause a ripple effect that went way past a single person who'd bullied me. We'd turned over the recording to give Miles the chance to get justice for what had happened to him, but actually, we'd inadvertently made his life a whole lot more difficult.

The attack had been a low-level dope exchange gone bad, and as more of the story came to light over the following weeks, the number of people involved grew and included some of the people Miles ran with.

Miles was expelled from Chesterford Academy, mainly because of the attack on Jonah, but add in the dope issue, and the knife, and that was his time with us done. Last we heard, he and his family had moved to his mom's place in Switzerland, so I doubted we'd see him again. School was quiet for a while, heading up to Valentine's, and the obligatory dance event in the school gym. The last time I'd been in here with it all fancied up with balloons had been for Halloween, and it was amazing how much had changed since then. Miles was gone. His beefed-up football cronies were quiet. The school had a brand-new policy on bullying that was basically one strike and you're out, something that having money at a private school could not get you out of.

It was a start.

"Ready to go in?" Felix hurried to my side, his costume nothing more than shirt and jeans in icy bitterly windy February. Someone—God knows who —had decided the Valentine's Dance would be summer-themed. How in the gods' names that had passed anyone's scrutiny, I didn't know, but at least I was wearing a heavy coat over my summer clothes. As was Jonah, who had his arms around me from behind and exuded warmth like a radiator. Soren was right on Felix's heels, Shaun next to him, both of them coatless as well.

Idiots.

"I was ready ten minutes ago," Jonah muttered.

I leaned back for an awkward upside-down kiss. "Let's go in then."

Soren and Felix went in first, Shaun with them, then the rest of the Coyotes, who'd all had more sense and waited for the big hockey entrance to the event inside the building. Then, it was our turn, but Jonah tugged me to the side, and then, in the opposite direction to the back corridor.

"Oooh making out by the lockers, in a quiet dark hallway," I mused. "I could get with that."

"We're not doing that." Jonah seemed determined, then halted. "Wait, what am I saying." He pressed me against the nearest locker, 813 I saw, and we kissed for a long time, wrapped in each other's arms, lost in the kiss, until someone cleared their throat behind us.

"Gentlemen?" the voice said—a familiar voice— Jonah's dad, who was here as a chaperone. "Wondered why you didn't come in with the team Tyler."

"Oops," Jonah said, and when his dad raised an eyebrow, Jonah grabbed my hand and we ran farther down the corridor, him dragging me, and me going wherever he took me. We ended up deeper in the school, taking a few lefts and rights until I was completely turned around, until we stopped running, and I realized we were in the science block.

"Okay, I need to tell you something," Jonah blurted and dropped my hand. "And you have to promise not to be mad."

I smiled up at my boyfriend. "You could never make me mad. Well, apart from the cheese on the popcorn thing." I winked at him, because we could tease each other for hours over what is and isn't appropriate to add to cinema popcorn, and we did, and it always ended up with more kissing.

"Well, you're the odd one out not liking that," he defended with the standard script, but then, he stopped teasing and instead took a step away from me. "Promise me you won't get mad, or react badly, or think less of me."

We didn't have many secrets the two of us. We talked about everything, from his family to mine, and all the things in between, about bullying, and being bullied, and regrets, and happy parts, and sad parts. In between kissing that is, because I really liked the kissing.

"I promise." It was an easy thing to say. "I love you," I added, and his smile reappeared for a moment.

"And I love you too," he said back, and I took a

step toward him for the kissing that needed to be happening right now.

"No. Stay there," he said, then tapped something next to him. I glanced down to see the suggestion box, the one where complaints ranged from exactly how many burgers we were restricted to, right up to the complaint that had gotten Jonah in trouble at the beginning of our story.

"What's wrong?" A panic circled my chest—was he breaking up with me? Was this the end before we'd even begun? Was I being dramatic?

"It was me," he said and tapped it again. "I was the one who put the complaint in about me and Miles."

I blinked at him. The thump of music in the building seemed to synch with my heart.

"I don't understand."

"I was so scared, Ty," he began. "I couldn't see a way out. I couldn't get away. I was desperate, and I knew what it would do, how it would put the spotlight on me, but I was messed up, and in a spiral I couldn't see a way out of."

"That's the bravest thing I've ever heard—"

"Don't say that." Jonah sounded miserable. "If I'd stayed quiet, then you wouldn't have been even more of a target for Miles and—"

I stepped right up to him and placed a hand over his mouth. "That was the bravest thing you could have done. You owned what happened; you became a target; your honesty got you punched in the face for protecting me."

"You don't hate me for painting a target on your back?"

I cradled his face, pressed a quick kiss to his soft lips, then smiled up at him.

"I love you. I admire what you did. You're mine. And I'm yours."

The kiss was easy, and the rest of our lives shone brightly, right there in front of the box that had started it all.

THE END

What's next for the Chesterford Coyotes?

Dance on Ice

Shaun & Kenji's story, coming Spring, 2024

mmhockeyromance.com/YANL

Harrisburg Railers

Owatonna U Hockey

Arizona Raptors

Boston Rebels

LA Storm

Chesterford Coyotes - Young Adult

Also By RJ Scott

For a full list of ebooks and links please scan the code
above or visit rjscott.co.uk/rjbooks

Meet RJ Scott

RJ discovered romance in books at a very young age and realized that if there wasn't romance on the page, she could create it in her head. With over one hundred and fifty books published, she is a full time author of gay romance.

She lives and works out of her home in the beautiful English countryside, spends her spare time reading, watching films, and enjoying time with her family.

The last time she had a week's break from writing she didn't like it one little bit and has yet to meet a box of chocolates she couldn't defeat.

www.rjscott.co.uk | rj@rjscott.co.uk

NEWSLETTER - rjscott.co.uk/rjnews

facebook.com/author.rjscott

x.com/Rjscott_author

instagram.com/rjscott_author

amazon.com/author/rj-scott

bookbub.com/authors/rj-scott

goodreads.com/rjscott

pinterest.com/rjscottauthor

Also By VL Locey

For a full list of ebooks and links please scan the code
above or visit vllocey.com/stories-from-vl-locey

Meet V.L. Locey

V.L. Locey loves worn jeans, yoga, belly laughs, walking, reading and writing lusty tales, Greek mythology, the New York Rangers, comic books, and coffee.

(Not necessarily in that order.)

She shares her life with her husband, her daughter, one dog, two cats, a flock of assorted domestic fowl, and two Jersey steers.

When not writing spicy romances, she enjoys spending her day with her menagerie in the rolling hills of Pennsylvania with a cup of fresh java in hand.

vllocey.com
vicki@vllocey.com

Newsletter - vllocey.com/newsletter

facebook.com/V.L.Locey

x.com/vllocey

instagram.com/vl_locey

bookbub.com/authors/v-l-locey

goodreads.com/vllocey

pinterest.com/vllocey